Embrace of the Wild

Inspired by equestrian explorer Isabella Bird

by,

Linda Ballou

Embrace of the Wild is an historical fiction novel inspired by equestrian explorer Isabella Lucy Bird.

ISBN: 9798702098043
Edited by Barbara Milbourn
Interior Design by formatting4u.com
Cover Image: Rich Briggs Photography
Cover art: Alexandra Corza

Published 2021 in the United States of America
Wind Dancer Press

What Readers Are Saying About *Embrace of the Wild*

"Reading this inspiring book makes me want to go out to the barn, saddle up and explore this wonderful world! This is one of those books that you would just love to see brought to life, Netflix, Amazon, check this one out!"

—Lisa Diersen, Director – EQUUS Film & Arts Festival

"Ballou sweeps you away with vivid scenes and characters of old Hawaii and Colorado, and bittersweet views of a changing world. But the real joy is riding with a recovered-invalid Englishwoman whose zest for life bursts from every page."

—Carole T. Beers, author of
New West Mysteries with Heart

"Fascinating portrait of Isabella Bird for those who love authentic historical fiction. Linda Ballou tells the truly amazing story of Isabella Bird, the British explorer in the nineteenth century in great descriptive detail."

—Rebecca Rosenberg, author of
Gold Digger-The Story of Baby Doe

"A GREAT story inspired by an AMAZING woman, British explorer Isabella Lucy Bird, Isabella's journey is told through her own eyes as she travels the world with wild abandon on the back of a horse, even finding peace and joy with a Colorado mountain man along the way. A wonderful ride!"

—Robin Hutton, author *Sgt. Reckless America's War Horse*

"The author skillfully puts herself in saddle of Isabella Bird and gives us a thumbnail sketch of what it took to launch the career of one of the greatest, most gifted, adventure travel writers of all time. Hold on for a wild ride and beautifully crafted descriptions of grand vistas, mountains, valleys and rivers most people will only dream about."

—Dr. Karen L. Moran, Pacifica University

Introduction

British explorer, Lady Isabella Lucy Bird (1831-1904) was one of the first cultural tourists, a free spirit, and beloved travel writer. Her mission was not to walk in the footsteps of famous explorers or literary figures, but to get to places others had not gone. She combined an anthropological interest with a need for adventure in her reflections on her journeys. Her books are compilations of her letters written to her younger sister Henrietta. In Hawai'i she learned that riding side saddle had exacerbated her life-long suffering from back pain. She broke the restrictive mold of the Victorian woman subjected to wearing tight corsets, strict repressive Evangelical teachings, and notions that a woman's place was in the home. No longer confined by chronic back pain, her maladies vanished. She became wild with her new freedom. Nothing less than climbing 14,259-foot Longs Peak in Colorado would satisfy her lust for adventure in the American West.

Her book, *A Lady's Life in the Rocky Mountains,* is the book that fired my imagination and inspired me to write *Embrace of the Wild.* In Estes Park, the isolated heart of the Rocky Range, she connected with the majesty in the "realm of the beasts." A middle-aged English woman traveling alone in the Wild West on horseback covering over 800 miles seemed an incredible feat. Her romance with Rocky Mountain Jim, a sympathetic, yet highly conflicted character added to the brew. My challenge writing her story in first person became keeping to the spirit of her letters without plagiarizing. Her descriptive powers are unrivaled. My humble attempt to step into her shoes will I hope be forgiven by anyone who has read her original journals.

Consummation of her romance with a trapper named James Nugent, aka Rocky Mountain Jim, was rumored but never confirmed. No one knows where Mr. Nugent came from or when he arrived in the Rocky Mountains. He was an alcoholic given to tall tales. He gave several versions of his origin, but none of them are verifiable. I took this opportunity to give him a history that reflected the times and fit with the story I wanted to tell. I placed him at the Sand Creek Massacre which was swept under the carpet by historians for many years.

In November 2000, the Sand Creek National

Historic site was established. The betrayal by Col. Chivington to Cheyenne peace chief Black Kettle at Sand Creek told the Indians that there would never be peace between "The People" and the whites swarming their world. After that they fought ferociously until 1866 when they were subjugated and removed to reservations by Union forces. I wanted to give a voice to the Native Americans through his character. I also tried to illuminate the settlers' side of the Indian wars.

I am an adventure travel writer by trade. This woman's beautiful writing and epic adventures far surpass anything I might hope to do. Her ability to blend in with the humblest conditions, to endure incredible hardships, and override the physical limitations of her frail body are unmatched. She became the most popular travel writer of her time. She remained true to her Christian upbringing doing charitable work throughout her life and giving all the profits of her books to others in need.

Part One

Island Magic

1873

Island Magic - 1873

Twenty brown skinned women astride sleek ponies thundered around the Honolulu quay. Their glossy black tresses flew in the wind with brilliant yellow and crimson dresses billowing behind. Frail health prevents me knowing such excess. I leaned over the railing of the Nevada as it made its way to the dock and reveled at their freedom of flight. The sight of them quickened my pulse and stirred the restless animal inside me that yearned to escape a lifelong prison of pain.

When I was a child, my father, who was a respected clergy, took me on his rounds to neighboring parishes seated on a pillow in front of him. I loved riding with him on his handsome Morgan, sitting side saddle like a lady. When we stayed at my grandfather's farm in the green hills of England, I was given a striking black gelding named Buttons to ride. I remember flying over meadows framed in row hedges down to a pond shaded by willows. There the horses were given rein to graze while we picnicked on the lawn. Those were the happiest days of my childhood. I never rode astride. Ever. It was not proper for a lady of breeding to spread her legs and her skirts in such rash abandon.

Now, paddlers with glistening arched backs powered their outriggers over the frothy surf to accompany us to shore. A reef surrounding the quay slowed the foaming rollers and formed a beach of powdery white sand. The women on horseback chased by their beaus had disappeared and the village came into view. The homes lining the bay were simple replicas of English cottages shrouded in shaggy palms. Clusters of humble thatched-roof huts housed the natives. All enjoyed extended verandas, or lanais, for evenings under a tapestry of stars cooled by a sultry breeze off the sea.

Hundreds of natives smiling with lustrous brown eyes and straight white teeth came to greet us eight sea-weary passengers. An aromatic garland of flowers was placed over my head by a lithe maiden wearing a colorful sarong with a flower design. She planted a gentle kiss on each of my cheeks. I was touched by her genuine welcome. These people display a happy countenance unlike the pinched faces of the cold, grey island I call home.

"Aloha," called our hosts as they collected our baggage and led us to a horse-drawn carriage. We were whisked to our hotel sheltered beneath the protective arms of a giant banyan tree. A winding path bordered with fanning ti plants, giant frilly ferns, and burning torches led to the hotel's main entrance framed in the gaudy magenta blooms of bougainvillea. Floors of rich burnished koa wood were covered in woven mats. All doors opened to the lanai letting in the flower-scented air. So inviting and gracious is this place that one can't help but put their cares aside and sink into the soothing calm.

"May I take you to your room madam?" A Chinese man in meticulous white trousers and jacket buttoned to his throat addressed me at the door. It appeared the servants were of foreign lineage, be it Oriental or perhaps some far-off island in the South Seas.

The voyage from Liverpool to New Zealand was peaceful until I reached the dusty shores of Auckland where I had the misfortune of boarding the Nevada. It was the only ship sailing to San Francisco via Hawai'i on the Web line delivering mail in the southern outposts. From there I intended to take a train to Colorado. I yearned to know more of America's Wild West. The Nevada was a huge paddle steamer in dilapidated condition. She had a decided list to the port, her crank was bandaged, she was leaky, and her mainmast was sprung. I wanted to get on with my journey so I took the chance we would make it. We learned too late that on her last journey she had nearly floundered, and the passengers unanimously signed a protest against her unseaworthy condition. The eight passengers boarding her could only pray that she was sound enough to get us to San Francisco.

The first day out of the Auckland harbor there was a shower that sent water into the salon. Water rose between the planks on the floor. We were obliged to wear rain jackets and rubber boots to dine. Cramped sleeping quarters were shared by cockroaches of prodigious size and a brazen rat population.

On the second day, we were hit by a South Seas hurricane that lasted twelve solid hours. The engine of the Nevada labored mightily as we listened to the thud of the sea pounding on the guards. She groaned and strained. The captain had lashed himself to the mast to avoid being swept overboard. If the engine floundered, we would surely be pounded to bits and succumb to a watery death. We passengers huddled together soundlessly as there was no point in trying to talk over the roar of the raging winds. It was an awful shrieking like a protracted scream of a woman being assaulted.

As the Nevada shuddered and lurched forward, we were left with nothing to do but pray.

I recalled the day I determined to do as doctors suggested and take a sea voyage to ease my maladies. When Papa passed away, Mama, my younger sister Hennie and I moved from the Wyton rectory in the south of England to a house in Edinburgh. Within the year, mother had joined my father on the other side. Rain splattered on the leaded glass window. My spirits were as sodden as the wet, grey world outside. The chill damp of northern Scotland settled into my bones making my back ache. My head throbbed with a ringing sound that gave me no peace. Jangled nerves forced me to take medicine to rest. I found myself profoundly bored with the life of doing good deeds for the poor and continuing the fight for temperance my father had started. Memories of my past explorations in the New World floated through my mind. My happiest times were when I was traveling, breathing in new sights and experiences. Even being pinned to the wall of my bunk on a steamer in the raging storm from Canada to Portland, Maine in gale force winds was better than being chained to the couch. I had a small inheritance, so I decided to see how far it would take me from this life not of my making and to strike out on my own. Finding myself in this predicament on the Nevada was not the expected shift of mind but, in a way, I was grateful for the trauma. It lifted me out of self-absorption and delivered me to stark terror.

The storm had finally subsided and then, at a most untimely moment, the only son of Mrs. Dexter began spitting up blood. He fell into a fevered state requiring careful nursing and incessant fanning. Each of the passengers took turns administering aid and trading shifts for the rest of our time together. I came to feel a special bond with my fellow passengers who proved themselves to be stalwarts in the storm and caring for one another.

"Miss Bird, may I call you Isabella?" Mrs. Dexter asked, her puddle-brown eyes ringed in red from too much crying.

"Of course, you may." Our intimate shared quarters for the past weeks negated formalities.

"The only hope for my son is that he be taken to the hospital in Honolulu when we make landing."

Her tears welled again as she prevailed upon me to accompany her when we made landfall. "I fear I will not be able to navigate my way in such strange surroundings," she said.

She was desperate with worry for her son, so I consented. It would not have been Christian for me to do otherwise. The thought of leaving the Nevada behind and spending time in the Sandwich Islands of Hawai'i filled me with a silent pleasure. San Francisco could wait.

Once docked and delivered to our hotel, I hired a carriage to take Mrs. Dexter and her son to the hospital. We careened through the bustling downtown of Honolulu past the plantation-style hotels lining the turquoise bay. The hospital was staffed with Chinese workers in crisp white uniforms. A kindly doctor who appeared to be of Japanese descent took the boy into his care. Mrs. Dexter chose to stay at a hotel nearby the hospital and I returned to my lodging.

French doors opened to a private lanai off my room. The four-poster bed with elaborate carvings on the headboard was covered in a handsome quilt with an explosive floral design of taro leaves brightened with red blossoms. I quickly attended to my toilet and sank into the feather mattress to a laborer's dreamless sleep. Beneath the mosquito netting draped from the ceiling to the floor I received my first full rest in recent memory.

I awoke to the sound of cooing doves, a rooster crowing, and the patter of a gentle rain on the glistening leaves of the ti plant outside my window. A platter of sliced mango, papaya, banana, and strawberries served with warm muffins and robust coffee awaited guests that included my fellow passengers in the dining hall.

"It looks to be a perfect day to explore the Island," said a Hawaiian man with almond skin, full lips, and tattoo of shark teeth that reached up his arm. He wore a cotton shirt with a feather fern design and crisp white pants. The warm rain had stopped, leaving a striking rainbow spanning the emerald green pali (cliffs) framing Manoa Valley. He offered to take us on a tour of the island of Oahu. I decided to seize this opportunity to acquaint myself with the island beauty before me.

Perched in the horse-drawn carriage driven by a native who only spoke Hawaiian and our host who spoke fluent English, I felt my senses quicken to the scent of plumeria and the sight of bright red blooms of the o'hia tree. Trailing liana vines wound around the trunks of immense banyan and breadfruit trees shading the well-traveled, rutted Pali Road. Expansive homes hidden in the thick verdure competed for the most elaborate gardens. One exotic oasis displayed a waterfall spilling over a rock ledge into a pool graced with elephant ear water lilies sporting flamingo pink blooms. Many have vegetable gardens with all manner of fruit and edibles.

Our host pointed to Queen Emma's palace, which to my standards was a humble structure sporting the grandest garden of tropical plants imaginable. Plumes of red torch ginger, orange and red swords of heliconia, and multi-colored bromelia were just a few of the exotics on display. Emma was the wife of Kamehameha IV. She had ventured to England and was befriended by Queen Victoria who sent her many gifts for her cottage including a cradle for her infant son who died at age four. Captain Vancouver made landfall on the Sandwich Islands in 1791 bearing gifts that included long-horned steers. He befriended Kamehameha the Great by interceding in a quarrel taking place with his favorite wife Ka'ahumanu. In return, Kamehameha allowed Vancouver to plant the British flag in the Islands. Even though there is much controversy over the validity of this claim by the English, Hawaiians are exceedingly proud of this connection with the Mother Country.

Our carriage on the dirt road to the Pali was overtaken by fifty-some horsemen and women streaking by us at a heart-catching pace. The women, girls, men, and boys rode as though they were on a steeple chase. The women were barefooted, sitting astride massive Spanish saddles wearing jangling spurs strapped to their ankles. Urging their mounts to full rein, they flashed by in a blur of crimson and gold. The men were no less vibrant with bright flower bands on their woven hats and red blooms ringing brown throats. I could only dream of what it must be like to join their cavalry as they left us stunned in their wake. I ached to join them, but the jostling ride on the rutted road through the forest triggered the familiar ache in my back that had kept me from such freedom.

When we reached the infamous Nuuanu Pali, we left our carriage to walk the hundred yards to a precipice with a staggering view of the crenelated pali of the Kualoa Range. Massive dark clouds engulfed the peaks that looked like jagged shark teeth piercing the heavens. White streams flowed in the creases of the mountains sheathed in lush green. I could see traces of steep trails descending the peaks that only a fool would attempt. The sun cast a shaft of light on the shimmering Pacific in the distance leaving a lake of platinum shine. This was the spot where Kamehameha the Great, the first ruling chief to unite the Hawaiian Islands, pressed his enemy, the ruling chief of Oahu, over the precipice along with hundreds of his defending men and women warriors. Our host explained how Kamehameha declared himself king and became the genesis of the royal lineage ruling today. The winds eternally whip this spot of infamy. There is an eerie swirl of spirits that never leave.

Upon returning to our lodging, I was cornered by my breakfast companions, Mr. and Mrs. Damon.

They had met a young American woman eager for a companion on a sailing venture to the volcanic island of Hawai'i. They assured me that she was a worldly traveler and would be the best of company. I was intrigued by the myths of Pele, the haughty goddess who rules over the largest active volcano in the world. The prospect of seeing the earth in its primal state intrigued me.

"The Kilauea sails in two hours," said Mrs. Damon. "Miss Karpe has arranged a carriage to take her to the dock. It could prove to be a most exciting adventure. I wish I could go, but we are leaving the Islands in the morning."

"Two hours! But I've no riding gear nor saddle," I said.

"Guides will provide you with horse and saddle and whatever you may need," she assured me. "The boat only sails once a week."

I feared I was not fit enough for the horse trek up the flank of the volcano but pressed those doubts aside. I'd lost too many years confined to the couch. I couldn't refuse this chance for a real adventure. The Dexter boy was in good hands, and the Nevada would be in dry dock being repaired for at least a week.

"Alright then, I'll go."

"Get packed and I will let Miss Karpe know you will be joining her," said Mrs. Damon.

My heart raced as I hastily packed a bag then boarded the waiting carriage pulled by two prancing white horses dressed in collars of red roses.

"I'm so glad you decided to join me," said Miss Karpe, a comely young woman with marble skin and crown of red curls who awaited me in the carriage.

"Thank you for the invitation," I said, secretly hoping to myself I would not be an impediment to our adventure.

"What brings you to the Islands?" she asked.

"A serendipitous circumstance left me free to join you. I had no intentions of going to the Big Island as they call it here, but I have read about the volcano. The opportunity to view the living caldron was irresistible."

It was a frenzied decision, but when we arrived at the wharf all apprehensions disappeared. I felt like Cinderella being whisked to the ball incognito.

Sail to Hilo

The wharf was dense with clamoring natives hugging and kissing as though they would never see one another again. The deck of the Kilauea was crowded with men, women, and children garlanded in scented flowers who were laughing and gesticulating in exaggerated manner. Their accompanying dogs, cats, fibrous mats, calabashes, bananas, and dried fish left little room for me to find comfort. I eventually found a seat leaning against one of the massive Spanish saddles stacked along with bridles, stirrups, halters, reins—all manner of tack that I came to learn was essential gear for the Hawaiians.

As we steamed out of the harbor, friends and families on shore waved and cheered as though the Kilauea was taking out on a world voyage. I was glad to see the busy hub of Honolulu fall away. I hoped to know the beauty of the Islands in their natural state without the stamp of humankind. The deck was covered with mats on which the nearly two hundred natives sat, ate, and smoked. They chatted endlessly amongst one another while sharing their provisions. Often, they broke into song accompanied by a stringed instrument called a ukulele and a drum made from a gourd. I was struck by the melodiousness of their deep-throated voices.

Miss Karpe had procured sleeping quarters below deck for the two of us. I visited her cabin and determined it would be a sweltering bed akin to a slave rack. When I spied a cockroach the size of a mouse skittering across the bedding, the issue was settled for me. I preferred to join the locals on deck and was offered a mattress on the skylight which suited me nicely.

The Kilauea is a tested vessel—sound, with no hint of luxury. It churned slowly but surely over the rolling swells of the deepest blue. Dolphins rushed ahead surfing in waves curling off the bow. Night fell with a searing red sunset casting pink and orange streaks on the metallic sea. Soon, a velvet canopy overhead sprinkled with stardust and a warm trade wind was our company.

From my skylight perch, I recognized Bishop Willis, a guest at my hotel, lying on a mattress among the locals. He waved to me to join him.

"What brings you to Hilo, Miss Bird?" he queried with what I perceived as genuine interest in the English woman traveling alone.

"I am drawn by the myths of Pele, so I seized upon the opportunity to know the power of the volcano first-hand," I replied.

"Ah, well, hers is a pagan power that still holds a charm over the natives. Do you know the many stories that have been handed down about her jealous heart?"

"No, but to hear them would help pass these hours," I said, delighted to have the distraction.

Bishop Willis is a born storyteller; a kindly man whose mischievous blue eyes and bushy brows reminded me of Grandfather Bird. I spent many happy hours with my grandfather. He told me of his travels to the colonies in India and Africa and read stories to me about early explorers. I could only read dreamy books of exotic faraway lands when I spent summers on his farm in the Cotswolds. There was a world globe in his study that I could spin, close my eyes and stop it by putting my finger on a dot that I would then explore in his expansive library. I was not allowed to read fiction at home, so I read books by the fire in Grandfather's study. Charlotte Bronte's, *Jane Eyre*, the story of a girl who demanded respect was one of my favorites.

As I grew older, Grandfather could see that I was chafing at the bit under the thumb of my father's strict Evangelical teachings. One day he took me aside and told me the dark secret of my past.

"Your father was not always so pious and bent on practicing self-denial. In fact, he was quite the man about town and a barrister with a promising career. Like me, and I think you, he had a thirst for travel and a curiosity about the wider world. What you don't know is that he also had a family before he married your mother. He took his first wife Emma, a vibrant young woman of seventeen, to India with him where he planned to seek his fortune. She bore him a precious son, but when the bubonic plague struck British India, it took both their lives. Edward blamed his sensual appetites and material desires for their deaths. He became a man of God as his penance."

Stunned by this revelation, I did not know what to say. I went to the paddock, gathered some brushes, and went to Button who was grazing peacefully. I hugged his muscled, warm chest and kissed his velvety nose. I brushed his forelock and scruffy mane and tail until they were free of tangles. Tears streamed freely while I curried his black coat until it shined. My father had deceived us. I was being punished because of his misdeeds, not mine! I had always suspected that he had wished for a son and that I was a perpetual disappointment to him. I lay my head on Buttons' side soaking in his warm strength and cried until the tears would come no more.

Hennie, my younger sister, and I were directed to do charitable works for the people in Father's parish. I rode to the villages he served as his representative. There was some joy for me working in the church bazaar to raise funds for those less fortunate, but it was not the work I wanted for myself. Father was determined that I would not succumb to worldly endeavors or carnal pleasures. Now, I knew why he kept me and Henrietta from knowing the powers of the flesh and vain worldly pursuits, but I also knew that I was a Bird, and that travel was in my blood.

It was not until I met my Aunt Barbara when I was twenty-one that I dreamed of becoming a writer. She was my mother's sister, disowned by the family because of her willful ways. My father, concerned with my continued headaches, fatigue, and insomnia decided I should go to London and seek the opinions of the best medical doctors. My mother, determined that I should find a husband to be devoted to, agreed that time spent with Uncle Lawson would be beneficial. He owned a manor in Kensington and enjoyed an active social life. My aunt, Barbara Lawson, came to visit her brother while I was there.

One would never know she was related to my mother who took pride in maintaining a respectful, austere manner. Aunt Barbara's auburn hair was in an upswept do and she wore a jaunty riding habit. She flashed an easy smile with sparkling blue eyes glittering with intelligence, and then she greeted me with a shocking hug that made me blush. At that moment it dawned on me that my mother, who woke Hennie and me every morning at dawn to get down on our knees to pray, never hugged me.

"I've longed to meet you in person," Isabella," she said.

I had no knowledge of her desire to know me. I only knew that she was not welcome in our home. There had been a break between her and my mother because of her defection from the church before I was born. Her name was never mentioned.

"I can't wait to show you the sites in London!" she exclaimed.

I followed her energetic, confident stride through Regents Park to the Tower of London; the British Museum where Egyptian mummies, Roman friezes, Greek statues, and other treasures from ancient cultures reside; and on to Buckingham Palace. One brilliant day she took me to the theatre where we saw a Shakespearian production. Afterwards, we had coffee with a bevy of her literary friends. They were an eclectic mix with outlandish, almost clownish attire. It was so exciting to be among people who loved to read and who had all manner of opinions about books and authors.

Aunt Barbara made her living writing articles. I asked her where I might find them to read. Aunt Barbara told me she wrote under the pen name of Paul Roberts. She said it was necessary to get published. It didn't seem to trouble her that that is what she had to do to make a living in a man's world, but it bothered me tremendously. Why should she have to hide her beautiful mind?

At the train station she bussed me on both cheeks in the European way. Hot tears of gratitude welled. In a too-short week she had opened my eyes to endless possibilities.

"Remember, Isabella, don't be afraid to be yourself," she said giving me one last hug.

The Kilauea lurched over a swell slamming down hard bringing me back to Bishop Willis and his lulling voice as he continued to "talk story."

"Pele resides in Halema'u ma'u Crater, a bubbling mass of lava inside the belching heart of the volcano. She holds the power of destruction and renewal in her hand. It is prudent to offer her *ohelo berries* before you dare to look into her blazing eye."

"Ah, and where might I gather such berries?"

"They are blue and grow on bushes. Look for them on your ride up to the crater."

"Pele is a jealous goddess given to rage," he continued. "There are many stories of her epic struggles with her sister Poliahu, the snow goddess who resides in Mauna Kea. They battle over their mutual lover Kamupua, a god who is half man and half pig who wears a long cloak to cover his hairy back. He is a potent warrior of intense passions. Legend has it that in these battles over their mutual lover, Poliahu defeats Pele's molten rock showers with her great white cloak of snow."

"How do you come to know these tales?"

"I have lived among the natives for three decades. The people serve Christianity, but the pagan fires still burn in their hearts. They fear the gods of old. Pele once had her own following who pledged loyalty only to her. It is said that if a child wandered into their midst, it would be taken and never seen again. Her cult is still feared."

"If that is so, should I be afraid?"

"My goodness, no," he chuckled. "I've not heard of any abductions in recent years, but Hawaiians say they have met Pele on the roads. She disguises herself as a crone and travels with a little white dog. They still believe in her unchecked powers."

"Do you have lodging in Hilo?" he asked.

"No, I came on short notice. I am traveling with Miss Karpe who is sleeping below. She will require lodging as well."

"There are no hotels in Hilo. You may stay at

my home if you wish. I will arrange a guide to take you ladies up the flank of the volcano to lodging at the Crater House."

"Most kind of you. I am truly grateful for your hospitality."

"It is the Island way," he said simply.

After nearly three days of sailing on deep rolling swells, we landed in the endearing village of Hilo. It was a most joyous greeting as though we were carrying royalty onboard. Miss Karpe finally emerged from below deck with bloodshot eyes and a pale pallor. It was difficult not to wince when looking at her weary expression. We were ferried to the dock in a whale boat and unceremoniously hoisted ashore by a husky brown native. Dark-haired girls and boys galloped on horseback along the white sand wrapping the azure crescent bay fringed with palms. Both the boys and girls were gaily festooned with flowers on the band of their hats and around their necks as I had seen in Honolulu. Swimmers on surf boards and others paddling canoes all came out to welcome the Kilauea. Gentlemen in white linen suits representing the missionaries were eager to greet us and shake our hands. Natives met their fellows with alohas of nose rubbings, kisses, leis of flowers, and feathery fern crowns. A bevy of children circled Bishop Willis who tossed them treats from his backpack.

Miss Karpe and I were soon delivered to Bishop Willis's plantation house that had two deep verandas framed in lattice ensconced in vines with a profusion of aromatic blooms. Palms swaying in a sweet breeze offered shade from the tropical sun. Bishop Willis introduced us to his wife Kala, a native woman of prodigious size. She wore a floor-length night shirt called a mu-mu and flowers in a mass of billowing black hair streaked with gray. Her movements were graceful and flowing as she served us refreshments on the veranda while the sun slipped behind a velvet green pali and cast a crimson glow over Hilo Bay. Miss Karpe rocked peacefully in a wide-winged wicker chair fanning herself lightly. She had green eyes flecked with gold beneath long lashes, red hair in an upswept do like Aunt Barbara's, ivory skin unbranded by the sun, and hands that have not seen labor that marked her a lady of means.

"Where do you hail from Miss Karpe?" queried Bishop Willis.

"I am from Colorado; Denver to be exact," she replied.

"What brought you to Hilo? We don't often receive ladies traveling alone."

"To be honest, Mark Twain sparked my curiosity. I was inspired by his letters from the Sandwich Islands. He said that "Hawai'i is the prettiest little archipelago ever to lay anchor in the South Pacific."

"Colorado was recommended to me by my doctors," I volunteered. "Edinburg is so cold and dreary in the winter. It serves to depress me. I know of many who have gone to Denver for the cure."

"Yes, the dry, thin air can help those suffering from consumption and other maladies, but I crave the moisture of the tropics that is blessed with extravagant life and the sea breeze," Miss Karpe followed.

"Indeed, I share your intoxication with this nurturing clime."

"Should you come to Colorado, I will see that you are well taken care of. My father owns a little goldmine in Telluride, and we enjoy company at our mountain home and in Denver."

"Thank you, that is most generous. I have read about the unrivaled majesty of your Rocky Mountains and would love to know Estes Park and surrounds. In fact, I have arranged for a mountain tour when I reach North America."

"When you arrive at Longmont, which is the gateway to the Front Range, please say hello to the Bakers for me. They are a lovely English couple who run the only civilized establishment within miles of Estes Park.

"Once you enter Estes Park, you are bound to

meet Rocky Mountain Jim. He is a quixotic character who fancies himself the guardian of the mountains. His bouts of debauchery in Denver are legendary."

"Thank you for the warning. Should I be frightened?"

"I don't think so. They say that if you treat Jim like a gentleman, you will find one. No one knows where he came from, but he does know how to pen a letter. Many of his editorials stating the case for preservation of the mountains have been published in the *Denver Gazette*. He is a trapper with a penchant for poetry and is quite popular with the old timers. But beware, he has a scandalous reputation with the ladies."

"I will keep that in mind when I meet him."

"You will not be disappointed with the mountains surrounding Estes Park, but I venture that the 14,000-foot peaks peering down on Telluride are as inspiring," Miss Karpe added.

"There is always more to see. I will do my best to take it all in."

"I hope you will share your adventures with me in letters, Miss. Bird. I've not been off Island for thirty years. I don't miss the harsh winters of New England and I am busy with my parish. I confess losing interest in the outside world, but I would like to know your impressions of what you see. Breakfast is served at eight ladies. I hope you get a good rest for your ride. I will see you in the morning," said Bishop Willis.

With that, we bid each other good night.

Before drifting to a dreamless sleep, I took a moment to write a letter to Hennie. I wanted to take note of all that had transpired in the last week and let her know of my detour in the Islands. Hennie, three years my junior, was the baby of the family with blonde curls and bright blue eyes. She filled the picture of feminine perfection: docile, obedient, cheerful, and kind. I, on the other hand, was full of constant questions that annoyed my parents greatly. I have small hands and feet, ears too close to my head, and teeth that protrude. Worse than any of those imperfections, I have a no-nonsense look about me that often threatens people. Hennie was always the favorite, but instead of sibling rivalry we only have love for one another. She gathered the letters I had written to her when I was on my tour of the east coast of the New World and fashioned them together for my first book *The Englishwoman in America*. She is such a dear soul, uncomplaining and dedicated to helping me publish my work. I asked her if she would like to accompany me on my first outing to London, but she said that she preferred to stay home and travel with me in my letters to her.

Breath of Pele

I awoke to delightful birdsong and the patter of a tropical rain on the leaves of the banana trees shading the garden outside my window. Bishop Willis kindly arranged for us to have two horses and a guide named Upa who spoke a smattering of English. He was picturesque in loose riding pants cinched with a rope tie and a garland of flowers on his wide brimmed hat. He also provided me with his daughter's flannel riding dress of the type the natives wore. I donned Turkish trousers beneath my borrowed dress, my dusty New Zealand boots, and the dog-skin gloves I acquired in Australia. It was a bizarre outfit but would serve the purpose.

Even though Miss K had suffered greatly from sea sickness, she was eager for our ride up the flank of the volcano. She appeared wearing a snappy riding habit with a waist-length waterproof and a broad-brimmed bonnet sporting netting to protect her from the sun. Using the mounting block to slide onto the side saddle she brought with her, she made an elegant picture.

My horse was a raw-boned gelding with a scruffy broom for a tail. His tack consisted of a huge deep-seated Mexican saddle with leather flaps, heavy wooden stirrups, and a bridle with a vicious curbed bit.

I told Bishop Willis that I had never ridden astride and feared the outcome of this indignity. Further, I prayed this new position would not be an insult to my back and exasperate its chronic ache.

"You will be glad for the deep seat of this saddle to remain secure on these rough trails that are pocked with potholes and deep gullies," he insisted.

When I had reached the age of sixteen, the fibrous tumor growing on my spine had placed such pressure on my sciatic nerve that it finally forced me to bed. All joy was taken from me and I could barely lift my head from the pillow. It was determined that I must have the tumor removed. The surgeon performed the procedure without chlorophyll or as much as a slug of whiskey. The pain was so excruciating that my entire being rebelled. My mind left my body and floated to the ceiling where I watched the doctor remove the offending growth. He did not cleanse the wound properly and it became infected and abscessed.

The recovery from the surgery took many years. I remained feeble for the rest of my teens. As I lay listening to birdsong outside my window yearning to ride again across the village greens, a deep melancholy set in. I became morose and inward trying to understand why God had stricken me. Why not take me to a sweeter place than leave me lying here in agony?

For many years I carried on, but depression driven by chronic pain took over my life. Kindly doctors tried everything in their medicinal arsenals, including the opium tincture laudanum, with no lasting results. It eased the pain but made me sleep; the days and months drifted by. When I was thirty-eight, all hope was lost. In a fit of genuine concern, my doctor created a metal brace for me to wear so that I might have strength in my spine to hold myself erect. This medieval instrument of torture served to compound matters carving deep grooves beneath my arm pits and lacerations where it rested on my hips. It made me as stiff as a fire poker unable to bend forward or twist to the side. I wore this unforgiving metal vest for two years. My muscles wasted and I became weaker still. I lacked all vitality and the will to live. I became like the consumptive parishioners I served unable to face another day of hopelessness. I rose before the pearly dawn, got on my knees and prayed as Mother made me do as a child, but instead of praying for the less fortunate, I prayed for my own demise.

Today was a new day. My desire to know the volcano won over my mortification of riding astride. I felt determined to reclaim my life! Most unlady-like, I attempted to mount by flinging my booted leg in the air to the other side of my horse. Untested leg muscles combined with my first attempt to straddle resulted in kicking the poor animal in the side. He side-stepped and swished his broom tail in indignation. The second attempt got me there with only a questioning equine glance. Seated in this unnerving but not unpleasant position, I said one last prayer blocking the fear that I would be sent spiraling backward into that pool of pain I swam in for so many years and hoping I would not have to resort to the bottle of laudanum I'd packed in my saddle bag in the event the pain became too intense.

The thirty-mile ride up the flank of the volcano proved to be a joint-pounding upward trajectory. Upa led us at a full gallop for the first three miles, careening through a dense forest that left me breathless. Ducking limbs of twisting trees draped in vines of exquisite green, I thankfully managed not to be decapitated. To stay mounted, I held with all my might to the saddle horn and gave the horse his head. He followed Upa through twisting turns splashing through rivulets and scrambling over rocks on the other side. When Upa pulled up short, I nearly flew over my horse's head and clung ignominiously to his mane. At that moment we came upon a bevy of native girls swimming in a rock pool who giggled at the predicament of the struggling haole wahine (foreign woman). Me.

We paused to let the horses catch their breath and to tighten their girths for the uphill climb to come. To my consternation, Miss K sat regally upright through it all, not a hair out of place. The respite gave me time to ponder the thick undergrowth in this burst of tropical jungle. Nature is given to excess in this hot-house environment. I recognize some of the plants that I have seen in a stunted version at the Edinburgh Botanical garden. There were palms and breadfruit trees, a maze of ferns and lianas, vines that wound around the limbs of the trees as thick as a man's arm. A canopy of giant banyan trees blocked the intense sun creating a cool Eden laden with the tender blue blooms of morning glory vines.

We remounted and Upa signaled us on with a slap on my horse's rump. A couple of hours later, we emerged from the dense green to a narrow track of no more than two feet wide over a ribbon of lava called pahoehoe. The surface was slick as a mirror and our horses slipped and floundered trying to find purchase. Leaving the forest left us to the mercies of a scorching sun upon a black expanse tufted with billowing gold grasses growing in cracks. A few ohi'a trees with flame-red blooms managed to cling to life here in the remnants of an epic explosion from the volcano.

We stopped at a halfway house where a ragged band of natives sat in the shade. An old man with scaly skin wearing a cloth thong called a malo stared at me with a jaundiced eye. The equally old woman in a kikepa made from a piece of tapa cloth tied at her shoulder stared too. They sniggered as Upa spoke to them in their native tongue. When I heard the words haole wahine I suspected they were talking about me.

Upon his return, he buckled a heavy, rusty Mexican spur with jingling ornaments and rowels an inch and a half long on to my boots. "You will need these to get him up the climb to come."

I hated wearing these instruments of torture, but I would come to understand that my horse was numb to gentler persuasions.

"What were they laughing about," I inquired.

"They wanted to know why you are here."

"I told them you are the representative of Victoria from the Cold Island come to know the breath of Pele."

"What! I am not a royal. Why did you lie to them?"

"I did not lie. That is what I was told."

It seemed the rumor about the village of Hilo was that I am a high chief related to Queen Victoria, who is held in high esteem by the natives. I decided to let the charade persist as it might work to my advantage when dealing with the natives.

The next five hours was a grueling scramble over a narrow rock-strewn trail. My muscles were mush, but the deep seat of the saddle miraculously kept me secure. With grim determination I pressed on. Even though the elevation is gradual (4,000 feet in the thirty miles) the trail goes up and down rock steps, through springs, and along narrow ledges. To add to the challenge, it began to rain. It was not a warm, tropical rain, but a drenching downpour. I had to constantly prod my exhausted horse to keep up with Upa and Miss K who seemed undaunted sitting erect with her umbrella overhead. Upa, wearing a poncho, trotted on at a merciless pace. I could only stay in the saddle by leaning on the horn. I would have gladly slept on the side of the track if Upa had let me.

The sun had set by the time we reached the Crater House, the only lodging on the rim of the caldera, still the sky was an ominous orange. Flashes of light pulsing from the pit of the volcano colored the sky. As we approached the house, I could see clouds of red sulphurous vapor mixed with flame curling out of the blackness that is Kilauea. At last, we had arrived at the largest active volcano in the world.

After tea and a warm-up by a blazing fire, Upa suggested that Miss K and I enjoy a makeshift sauna. He led us on a winding path through a belt of ohi'a where thin, thatched walls framed a steaming fumarole. He left us there to disrobe and sit on benches placed around the escape hatch of Pele's hot breath. Modesty dictated I leave on my undergarments which became thoroughly soaked in moments.

"Pretty sure sleep will come easy tonight. That was quite a ride," chirped Miss K.

The warmth soothed my aching limbs. "Yes, I hope to enjoy the sleep of the dead." So far, my back had not failed me. It felt like a miracle was taking place. That I had endured such a strenuous ride without ramifications seemed impossible. I did have my laudanum in case I had a relapse.

"Do you always travel alone Isabella?" she asked.

"Not in the beginning. On my first cruise in 1854 to the New World, my mother insisted I have a chaperone. She found it unseemly for a young woman of twenty-three to travel alone. The ruse was that I was to seek out friends of the parish and to gather information for my father's book about the revival of the Evangelical faith in the New

World. I knew this plot was hatched to dispel my melancholy. Mother agreed to it in the hope that I would find a husband. Father gave me a hundred pounds, letters of introduction, made arrangements for escorts, and told me I could stay as long as my money lasted, so I should use it wisely.

"Even though I had to attend 130 sermons and despised being supervised, that trip opened my eyes to many wonders. I sailed from Liverpool to Halifax on the Canada, a journey that took nine days and four hours. From there I traveled by boat, train, and cart from Canada to the slave waters of the Mississippi. I was totally enthralled by what I saw. I recall sitting in the wigwam on Prince Edward Island with an Indian woman who had just given birth to twins. I envied the simplicity of her life. No tight corsets, no clumsy bonnets, no calls to pay, no rector duties to perform, just living in the bosom of the natural world. New York was teeming with immigrants. Raw and murderous assaults took place there every night. I took a steamer on the Saint Lawrence River en route to Quebec that sailed through rapids and rocky escarpment. The journey buoyed my spirits and gave me fodder for my first book *The Englishwoman in America* and an addiction for travel and writing about my explorations. I determined to return and know more of the unbounded New World."

"And now you prefer to travel alone?" Miss K continued to press the issue.

"Yes. Travel is an elixir to my maladies. I am totally engaged when I am in the state of exploration. My senses become heightened. The voice of a fleeting bird, a pine-scented breeze, or the stir in the leaf litter made by a creature hiding from my eyes holds my keen attention. I don't choose the common destinations, nor luxuries, I prefer the unknown. It is a blessing to be so enraptured, but these pleasures are not easily shared with another. In fact, the presence of someone else can be an unwelcome intrusion. I write letters to my dear sister Henrietta who helps me organize my journals into books."

"Do you have children?" she asked with the bold innocence of an American.

"No," I said, not wanting to engage the subject.

"What about marriage?" Miss K asked with genuine curiosity.

I was taken back by her forthrightness. I had been taught that all of society believes a woman's sole goal should be to get a good provider for her eventual offspring. It was an audacious question, but I decided to give her my honest answer.

"If you want to be a vine clinging around a tree, then get married," I said.

At this revelation, a strained silence fell upon us putting an end to the inquisition.

I would like to have fallen into a deep sleep after my steam, but instead I woke disturbed by my recurring childhood nightmare. I have long suffered from insomnia. Satan seizes upon me, turns me upside down and stuffs me into an airless bag. I don't know why this imagining followed me here, but I woke up gasping for air.

"Isabella are you alright?" Miss K was standing over me looking down upon me with grave concern. I'm sorry, but I felt I had to awaken you from your nightmare. I could hear you moaning from my room."

"Thank you. I'm so sorry." I was drenched with sweat. "The steaming mists at the sauna must have brought Satan to mind. I've not had that dream since I was a child. Please go back to bed. I will be fine."

"Alright then, I will see you in the morning," said Miss K leaving me to stare into the dark until the gray light of dawn.

Hale-ma'u-ma'u, home of the fire goddess, was a three-hour march on foot across a stark lava field beneath a broiling sun. There is no guarantee of what the performance will be when you arrive at her home. Miss K and I stopped before departing from the Crater House to read entries in the Volcano Book where strangers from around the globe have written their impressions of their time here. The performance of the volcano is not static.

It can be a bubbling inferno, or a placid gray lake. Such remarks read:

Not much of a fizz.

Madam Pele in the dumps.

But then, "Look!" exclaimed Miss K with giddy excitement, "an entry from Mark Twain."

> *After we got out in the dark we had another fine spectacle. A colossal column of cloud towered to a great height in the air immediately above the crater, and the outer swell of every one of its vast folds was dyed with a rich crimson luster, which was subdued to a pale rose tint in the depressions between. It glowed like a muffled torch and stretched upward to a dizzy height toward the zenith... I was sure that I now had a vivid conception of what the majestic "pillar of fire" was like, which almost amounted to a revelation.*
>
> ~Mark Twain 1866

Soon, it was time to depart. We were given local guides with knowledge of the weak spots in the crust of the lava field. They spoke little English, but it was obvious they found our cumbersome garments comical. The tramp to Hale-ma'u ma'u begins with a trail that zigzags down the inside wall of the crater shaded by ohi'a trees and fanning tree ferns. I spotted the blue ohelo berries Bishop Willis told me pleases the moody goddess. I snagged a few for good measure. I am not superstitious and do not fear pagan gods, but I do respect the traditions set in place by those who do.

The crater floor was a swirling mass of black ribbons of lava. Noxious steam rose from vents beside the track. We marched single file behind our guides making certain to stay in the tracks as they tested the surface before us. Upa served as rear guard. I could feel the heat coming through the soles of my boots. The march took us over blocks of lava rock with ragged edges uplifted by many earthquakes and tremors. At one point I felt the ground trembling beneath me and feared a violent explosion that would send molten lava rivers down the flank of Kilauea to a steaming crescendo where it meets the sea. I tripped on a jagged ledge that took me off the path lined with rock cairn. I broke the fall with my hands at which time my thick dog-skin gloves instantly melted.

Ahead I could not see the pillar of fire Mark Twain wrote of and so prepared myself for disappointment. As we got closer, I heard a churning and spitting that sounded like waves battering a sea cliff. When we finally reached the lip of Hale ma'u ma'u, we ventured closer on a questionable ledge overlooking the lava lake below. I gasped at the overwhelming power of the Pele's cauldron. A shocking metallic crimson liquid bubbled and spurted in the boiling pot building enough force to shoot fiery columns of molten lava skyward. Unexpected tears flowed at the sight of the everlasting fires of hell, churning and spewing ceaseless waves of destruction. The proof of unutterable suffering lay before us. I shuddered in horror. Surely, this is the fate non-believers of the true God will meet; it is what my father had preached. Brimstone and eternal fire. I was not sure I shared his convictions, but I never doubted his sincerity. The ohelo berries tucked in my tunic filled my hand and I flung them into the awful inferno. I wished for myself the miracle of good health and that my mother and father both received the reward from their maker they had worked so hard to ensure. The heat was so intense my face began to blister, and I was forced to back away.

On the ride back to Hilo in the shade of the forest it came to me that what I witnessed was not a scene of desolation, rather one of creation. This island is built layer upon layer of raw, unformed material from the center of the earth. The volcano is the belly of glorious, mysterious, unfathomable beginnings; it was the source of all the abundant life around me. The horror that overtook me at the sight of the bubbling caldron was melting. I was grateful to have witnessed this miracle that words can't capture.

On the last three miles of the sixty-mile round trip, Upa gave free rein to the horses letting them careen over the narrow track at a full gallop. My feet, burdened by the heavy spurs, fell out of the wooden stirrups and I was upset from my seat. Dangling on the rump of my horse, I clung desperately to the rim of the massive saddle as it beat my chest mercilessly. I would not let go fearing a hoof strike to the head, or worse. There was no use crying for help, as Upa and Miss K sprinted far ahead of me. My brutish mount would not be denied his freedom to run home, so I held on.

When we finally reached the home of Bishop Willis, my legs buckled beneath me as I slipped down from the beast. My arms felt disjointed at the shoulder, knees screamed in agony, chest was bruised and battered, hands raw and blistered, and the tenderness of my bottom has no measure.

Upa came to me grinning with his white teeth. "I will take you to my Auntie Melanie. She will give you lomi- lomi in the hot pool."

I distrusted him now and hesitated to take him up on his offer but was desperate for relief.

Placing me behind him on his horse, he rode at a gentleman's pace to Auntie's thatched hut by the edge of the sea. Upa explained to her that I needed her remedy. She took my hand and guided me to Ahalanui Pond, a thermal pool warmed by the breath of Pele, known for healing powers. She was a large woman with a mass of wavy, gray-streaked hair framing her round face. She smiled at me with glistening brown eyes that held secret knowledge handed down to her by her elders. She stepped into the tepid pool extending a strong arm and guided me into the waters.

She told me to lie on my back and held me aloft with a strong, flat hand on my back. Her other hand she placed on my forehead and said a prayer.

"Blessed Akua give strength back to this little haole wahine who has traveled from the Cold Island to know your wonders. Spill your mana into her heart. Free her from the pain clustered in her body. Forgive her for not being a perfect child and open her heart to your loving touch. Amen."

I heard the waves crashing on the rock wall dividing the sea from the fresh water. The mixture of salt water and fresh creates a soothing elixir for body and mind. I grew limp as Auntie Melanie's firm hands administered the loving touch to my aching limbs. She swirled me in a circle around her and ended the session by pulling me in close to her ample breast and cradling me. Tears flowed unchecked at her tender mercies. It was as though the flesh was melting from my bones lifting a weight from my mind. The pain in my back that I have carried for so many years flew away like a white dove freed from a cage.

With my mind softened from water therapy, I was led to a mat in a thatched shelter that was open to a breeze off the sea. The warm air laden with ginger dried my wet skin. She combined long sweeping movements using her whole body to relieve the remainder of tension in my muscles and restore regenerative powers. She continued her supplications with long strokes of her forearm on each of my limbs, kneading with her elbows where she felt tension. To maintain my modesty, I was swaddled in cloth as she lifted my leg while bending my knee and rocking my leg in a circular motion from the hip. Next, she massaged sandalwood oil into the scars on my back and purple welts under my arms and on my waist—remnants of the brace I had worn for years. I found myself overtaken by heaving sobs. Never have I known such sensuality, such a sweet connection with my body. Cares flew away as I listened to the hiss of the waves receding over pebbles and dreamed of staying here forever.

Next day, I awoke once again in the home of Bishop Willis to the coo of doves and patter of the daily tropical shower on the banana leaves. The aroma of dew-laden flowers opening to the sun drifted through the open window. I felt tender but refreshed. The miracle was that I had no awareness of pain in my back! This must be a confluence of events that I would have to examine more closely. It seems that sitting side saddle from a young age may have worsened my condition while riding astride aligned my spine and left me free to ride for hours. It seemed a miracle was taking place.

The three of us breakfasted on papaya, guava, banana, mango, and pineapple slices garnished with lime juice and mint, toast and jam.

"I shall be returning to Honolulu on the next sailing of the Kilauea," Miss K announced.

Bishop Willis inquired of our previous day's experience and Miss K's plans in Honolulu. To me he said, "If you are staying on, Miss Bird, perhaps you would like to journey to Waipio, the Valley of the Kings. It is quite picturesque and is filled with myth and legends of the people of old. Bones of great chiefs are hidden in the pali and it is claimed to be the gateway to the underwater world of Po. The ride along the Hamakua Coast that delivers you there is an adventure itself."

"I would love to know more of the wonders

of Hawai'i! From the steamer I saw many waterfalls streaking the cliffs along the coast and would welcome the chance of a closer look."

"Good, then it is settled. I will arrange for Upa to take you along with his sister Kilani."

"Miss Karpe, perhaps you would like to meet some of my fellows in Hilo," he offered.

"Yes," she said, "I admit that I am missing society."

My thoughts were that she was more suited to city living and excited to be done with roughing it. I smiled to myself as this could be a perfect solution. Perhaps I would be offered Miss Karpe's more manageable mount; one that did not require a beating to move forward. The company of a female guide further absolved me of any improprieties.

Onward to Waipio

The next day broke fresh and clear beneath a lavender sky. I bid Miss Karpe adieu and a safe journey. She gifted me her riding gloves remembering that mine had melted during a fall, and she offered her umbrella as the ride to Waipio was likely to be wet. I wore my free-flowing flannel riding dress that did not bind my movements. After riding those grueling sixty miles to the crater and back, riding astride felt natural to me and did not trouble my back. The lomi-lomi massage had relieved the tenderness and burning sting in my muscles. I was ready for more, and decidedly more eager as the reins of Miss Karpe's horse were passed to me.

With his usual abandon, Upa led us on a merry romp on a narrow track for the first five miles. My cheeks flushed in the brisk wind as adrenaline charged through my system. We careened through tunnels of tree ferns and leapt logs in our path. Kilani wore a red rose crown on her hat, bright blue bloomers, and jingling spurs.

She was in the blossom of her youth and flashed laughing smiles at me over her shoulder. Her glossy black curls tumbled down her back as she rode effortlessly at full stride.

It is a sixty-mile ride to Waipio from Hilo on the King's Highway. In the days of old, the royals took their ease in the canyon that is protected on three sides by sheer cliffs and that faces a raging surf on the fourth. Here they could linger in peace and solitude away from the threat of their enemies. Foot soldiers once carried the messages of the royals to Hilo along this narrow track that traverses eight gulches.

Suddenly, Upa held his hand up signaling us to stop short. I stared over the edge of a chasm sheathed in deep green and questioned my need to reach the infamous Valley of the Kings. Without hesitation, Upa spurred his horse over the lip. Kilani followed. I had no choice but to spur my mount over the edge as well. The mare found footing and I leaned back on her haunches to help her gather her legs beneath her to navigate the steep decline. At bottom, we splashed through a stream running to the sea that had carved the corridor. I heard the thundering surf below as we charged the slippery incline back into a bright blue day. A cooling breeze off the azure sea visible through the palms made it a joyous ride.

Our pace was brisk as we trotted through dense forests of candlenut, or *kukui,* and breadfruit trees forming a silvery canopy overhead. Everywhere rocks and trees are ensconced in mosses and the ground is covered in exquisite ferns, from the delicate maidenhair to the hardy tree ferns. It is forest bursting with life. And what nurtures that life is rain. Dark clouds moved in with incredible speed and soon a deluge, not a gentle tropical mist, but a drenching rain came down in earnest. This was no match for Miss K's umbrella which blew out of my hands, and without a waterproof poncho, I was soaked in minutes.

Upa circled back, poked his head under my sagging hat, and smiled with his magnificent eyes. He was shirtless with a red sash around his waist and a *maile* of ferns on his hat. His brown, muscular frame glistened with vitality. He seemed always to be laughing at some inner joke. His graceful, effortless movements were that of a wild creature. He was impulsive and reckless. He is almost a complete savage with the exception that his skin was lighter than his brown brothers. He has a straight nose, a fine mouth with full lips, bright white teeth, and a mass of wavy black hair. He speaks enough English to get us by, but not enough to carry on gentle conversation. He is lovable in all ways except his miserable treatment of his horse which he handles in an extremely harsh manner. The poor animal is demanded so much of that its spirit seems nearly broken, yet it continues Upa's bidding.

"Cold?" he asked with a knowing grin.

"Wet doesn't bother me," I lied.

"We spend the night with my uncle," he announced.

After traversing four gulches, each one more precarious than the last, ten hours in the saddle, with the last hour in pouring rain, the thought of a meal and a roof over our head held great appeal. I envisioned steaming tea with warm scones awaiting us.

Upa's uncle's house turned out to be a dilapidated frame structure with two fenced piggeries. A toothless man emerged onto the lanai with a horde of scantily clad females standing behind him. We dismounted and were instructed to bring our wet tack into the 18 x 14 one-room hut. Deteriorating mats covered the floor. There were no coverings on the windows. We added our wet gear to the mounds of blankets, bananas, coconuts, *kalo* roots, and calabashes lying about in heaps. A frightful old woman with her body covered in tattoos huddled in the corner wearing only a ragged blanket on her shoulders.

Kilani offered me a dry cloth of kapa to be worn tied at the shoulder. Upa pulled off my soggy boots. Meanwhile, the old man killed a fowl and boiled it with sweet potatoes for our supper. They all spoke in their native tongue with the only recognizable words being haole wahine. I was likely the first white woman they have ever seen.

The food was spread on the mats on the floor. I sat cross-legged while the others lay prone. The starchy purple paste called poi is a staple served with every meal. They ate it with their fingers while I ate mine with my knife which garnered stares of curiosity.

"How old are you?" Upa suddenly asked with no apology for such a rude question. "They want to know." He waved to the audience of one man and four women.

With hand gestures, I indicated forty years.

"Too old!" he laughed as he shared this information with the group. They all sniggered at this revelation.

Too old for what, I wondered. To become a wife and brood mare for heathens? These people were just one generation from idolaters who worshiped blood-thirsty gods that demanded human sacrifice. Even though I could have spoken through Kilani who spoke English, I held my tongue. I was a guest grateful for their hospitality. Sleep came quickly even though I shared the room with seven strangers who continued to chatter well into the wet night.

In the morning I donned my still-damp riding habit. Upa helped me put on my stiff boots. The sun shone brightly and steam rose off the spreading ferns when we finally bid Upa's uncle farewell.

The rest of the journey to Waipio was uneventful save the crossing of the great Hakalau gulch. Here a wide river called for swimming. The booms that sounded like rolling thunder could be heard crashing on the shore of the sea just a hundred yards below. One could easily be swept away and pounded to death by the breakers rolling in from a 2,000-mile fetch. I pushed thoughts of disaster out of my mind as the mare struggled for traction. For a few fleeting moments we were swimming with the water over my waist until she found purchase and scrambled onto the slick, muddy shore.

We moved along at a single file trot for miles on a narrow track that opened to a clearing. Upa signaled us to halt and pointed to a herd of long-horned semi-wild bullock. Vaqueros they call *paniola* were herding the half-mad creatures that darted in and out of the brush. Upa said these herds are descendants of the gift that Captain Vancouver gave to Kamehameha the Great when he planted the British flag here in 1794. Dangerous and to be avoided.

The ride was without further incident until we reached the precipice overlooking Waipio Valley. The fertile valley was watered by a winding stream that sparkled with fishponds. A patchwork of kalo, oranges, coffee groves, figs, breadfruit, and palms covered the broad valley floor. A neat cluster of grass houses and a church with a spire formed the centerpiece. The head of the valley was crowned with a three-tiered waterfall cascading down the sheer cliff wall. The one precipitous track into the valley—the one we were on—was deeply rutted and soggy, so I dismounted and led my exhausted mare down. Upa gave no thought to the horses which were quite worn and spurred his mount. Kilani was no less cruel. It is ironic that such sweet, generous people in all other ways show no care for their animals.

Halemanu, a man of distinction and property, greeted us at the valley floor. Nearly seven feet tall, he held an imposing presence. His statuesque height marked him a descendant of the Ali'i, or royal class, evolved through centuries of in-breeding. His movements were graceful and light for a man his size. Intense and lustrous dark eyes buried beneath a thick black brow implied keen intelligence. Though he did not speak English, he was of good manner. I gave him my letter of introduction from Bishop Willis. He spoke to me though Kilani.

"You are most welcome here in Waipio. Your horse will be tended and you shall dine with me and my family this evening. We will make luau for you."

Our lodging was luxurious, especially in comparison to last night's comforts. My grass house with a lanai shaded by palms enjoyed a sweet breeze thick with floral fragrance. I walked up the valley to get a closer look at the staggering cascade. If ever there was a tropical paradise, this sheltered valley in the shadow of these great cliffs qualified. I know the bones of great chiefs are buried in caves and in the walls that frame Waipio. The entrance to Po, the underwater world where spirits dwell when they pass to the other side, is located on the south side of the canyon. Some say this valley is haunted with ghosts that walk at night. The natives believe there is much mana, or supernatural energy, here. Indeed, there was a magical aura about the place.

Halemanu serves the one true god delivered to him by missionaries. He has a cook house with a native cook and dining room with everything in the foreign style. It was a delight to once again sit in chairs at a clothed table laden with napkins, knives, forks, and even a salt shaker. We were served a lavish meal of pork that had been steamed in an underground oven, a cornucopia of fruit, and, of course, the obligatory purple poi. Before we settled into our meal, Halemanu gave a blessing in his native tongue.

"I would love to ride to the base of the falls in the morning," I said.

"It is not advised. Recent rains have caused stones to slip and collide," he replied through Kilani.

"I may never be here again. I will be vigilant," I insisted.

"You will have to swim the river. There are many crossings."

"I am from Scotland, where it is cold and damp year-round. I am not afraid of getting wet."

"You are a persistent woman. I will not deny you." Halemanu laughed with good humor at my folly.

With that, he excused himself and joined his family. Such a strange dichotomy he embraces. I was amused that after our meal he took his repast with his family lying on the floor mat and eating with his fingers.

The day broke clear. Halemanu assigned his pretty daughter Leilani, a lithe teen, to be our guide. Kilani removed her boots to make fording the river easier and advised me to follow suit. Now I was in my stocking feet riding astride a Mexican saddle eager to swim in this river with my steadfast mare. Indeed, there were many river crossings with water to my waist. We rode without incident up the valley to a meadow sliced by a fast-running stream. Leilani held up her hand and instructed us to tether our horses.

"This is far as we go," she said.

"But we are not nearly to the base of the falls," I protested.

"It is a rough hike with swift water crossings. You will have to swim."

Not to be deterred, I tied my horse to the nearest acceptably sturdy tree and plunged into the river in full dress to show Leilani I was not afraid to swim. She sighed heavily at my display.

"Stones are loose from rains. I will go no further," she said.

Upa, Kilani, and I would continue without her. The tramp was a hard one with crossings through a strong current that nearly pulled me off my feet. Scrambling over mossy rocks and clinging to thorny vines I was bruised and bleeding by the time we reached the waterfall plunging into a deep pool. Cool spray filled the air with mist where the torrent falling from the precipice above landed in the fern-laden grotto.

Legend has it that the god Lono caught his wife here having a dalliance with another warrior in this pool. In a jealous rage he murdered her and her lover. For centuries, Lono was sentenced to wandering the heavens in a canoe with white sails trying to find his wife so that he might say that he was sorry. When Captain James Cook sailed into Kealakekua Bay in 1779, the natives saw his white sails and believed he was Lono—the wandering god returning home. It was Cook's decision to allow this charade to persist that ultimately culminated into his demise at the hands of the natives who gave him a royal welcome.

I craned my head to see a rainbow arcing in the sunlight at the top of the cascade marking the end of a glorious adventure. On the slog back, we heard a rumbling sound. Boulders tumbled from a great height taking out a nearby ohi'a tree in its path. It was a somber reminder that nature here is as treacherous as it is magnificent.

Leilani had waited for us and now led us on a wild ride back through coffee and kalo fields. I was one with my sturdy mare, riding barefoot with my hair loose and whipping in the wind. My cheeks stung and felt flushed and my blood was up. I was loving every second of being alive! I was part of the cavalcade I'd yearned to join. There would be nothing or no one that would ever stop me from knowing this raw freedom again!

Upon our return, Halemanu wanted to show me the *Puhaonua*, or place of refuge here in the valley of vanquished waters. It is built of immense stones weighing tons that are fifteen feet wide. The gates were always open to murderers or tabu breakers alike. If they could enter the compound before their pursuers caught them, they were safe. Defeated warriors that were fodder for human sacrifice, and women and children could find shelter here during times of war. If the priest performed certain protocols, the offender could be spared death and return to society without punishment. There are only two of these Cities of Refuge on the island of Hawai'i. I think Halemanu wanted me to understand that his culture is full of paradox. Within it are slaughter-loving gods demanding human sacrifice and a system that allows forgiveness.

Our last supper was a delightful meal of Oregon kippered salmon, kalo, yams, rolls, and rich coffee—a most considerate and gracious tip of the hat to my Scottish home. Our gentle conversation turned to sad truths. Our host's eyes filled with a terrible sorrow as Leilani shared his grief with us.

"Forty years ago, there were 1,300 Hawaiians living in Waipio, now there are only two hundred. Smallpox, venereal disease, and now leprosy have depleted our numbers," she said.

Halemanu's eyes moistened as he looked directly at me and said in English.

"Soon there will be no *Kanakas*." [Hawaiians]

Hilo or Bust

Ominous clouds swarmed overhead as we made our way up the rutted trail leaving Waipio to the ghosts that haunt the sacred valley. Eager to make tracks before the rain let loose, we galloped for miles slowing only to navigate two of the eight gulches on the way back to Hilo. Splashing through streams, scrambling up muddy walls and ducking low hanging branches was exhausting. Upa was relentless. He spurred his horse until its flanks were bleeding and beat it around the neck and face. Finally, the poor brute floundered and broke down beneath him. It simply could not go a step further. This combined with blinding curtains of water forced us to seek shelter for the night.

Once again, Upa's family opened their humble home to us. We were given a good meal and dried our clothes by the fire. I did not sleep well with the rain drilling on the tin roof of the hut but was grateful for shelter from the deluge.

"You and Kilani will go ahead. I have to find another horse," Upa told me.

"Why can't we wait here for you?" I felt a bit un-nerved that he was to part our company.

"You still have to pass Hakalau gulch. If you don't leave now, it will be too big water to cross."

Not wanting to spend another night with his family, I looked to Kilani.

"I am going with or without you," she said plainly.

I was shocked at her announcement. "But you were assigned to my safe-keeping."

"My husband is expecting me," she said without apology.

Newlywed, her ardor was so strong she would not be swayed by my protests. I had to admit she is a capable young woman and an excellent rider. I prepared my mount for the journey. Upa's uncle packed some coconuts in my saddlebags with a few other provisions. The drenching rain persisted. Without a waterproof this would be a slog to remember.

The narrow track was now slippery with red mud. My mare struggled for traction, her legs frequently sliding out from under her. Cascades streaking white down the cleft of the pali dislodged rocks that rattled down the mountain. At times, the rain was so dense I lost sight of

Kilani who forged ahead. We crossed several smaller gulches with rushing water up to my horse's belly without incident, but when we arrived at the lip of Hakalau I lost my conviction. Water broiling in its riotous rush to the sea had risen half way up the side of the water corridor. Limbs of trees and leaves swirled in a muddy chaos. The thunderous sound of breakers crashing on the sea cliffs filled me with dread. If I didn't drown in the river, I would surely be carried by it and crushed on the rocks by the pounding sea. I decided I would prefer spending a night in the rain on the shore over attempting this crossing.

Two native men on the other side of the raging torrent had lassoed the horse of a woman trying to reach the other side. With ropes tied to trees they were pulling her to the shore. Her horse floundered, falling backwards and the woman lost her seat and went into the brew as well. She clung to the horn of the saddle while her body caught in the current. With Herculean effort the men pulled the flailing animal to the shore. The horse found purchase and the woman was rescued.

Kilani was not dissuaded by the perilous crossing we had just witnessed. She stood on the edge of the gulch prepared to jump in to certain death. The men threw the lasso over her horse's head and she pressed forward. My heart was in my throat as I watched her being picked up by the roiling water and sent spinning downstream. I screamed over the wild chorus of the river for her to face the flow. She was attempting to cross sideways with her horse completely submerged except for its head. She managed to swing around to face the torrent and the men were able to pull them to the shore. The horse's eyes rolled white with fear and it snorted and puffed in its struggle to find footing on the slippery terrain. Kilani managed to gather herself back onto the horse as it lurched up the far bank of the river. I could only hope for her that her husband's affections would be rewarded in kind.

I made my decision not to follow her lead, but as I was about to turn back, a lasso was hurled around my mare's neck. Without so much as an "Are you ready?" I was pulled into the swirling drink. Instantly immersed up to my neck, I had no choice but to press forward. I spurred the animal beneath me with all my might. She was swimming toward the far side, but we were drifting towards the sea. I yelled for help, but my screams were swallowed in the roar. This looked to be a sad ending to my new-found freedom.

From shore Kilani screamed, "Spur. Spur. Spur." Both men were on the rope around my horse's neck. They secured their feet on boulders, circled the rope to a tree for leverage. After each pull, they gave my horse a small release so they did not choke her to death. The animal was gasping and whinnying from such effort and terror that I felt her entire body shake. Now I was lifted by the water out of the saddle. My arms felt like they were being pulled out of their sockets as I clung to the big horn of the Mexican saddle. The rain was blinding, my strength was failing, and I was about to let go and join the spirits in the underworld of Po when I felt the mare contact something solid. In a reserve of strength, she lurched forward. With the men still pulling, she was able to scramble up the slick wall of mud.

Upa finally arrived with a mule in tow. The men tossed him the rope that he put around the creature's neck. He deftly hopped rocks, dove into the muddy brew, and navigated the charging river like an amphibious creature leading the mule behind him. He laughed loudly when he reached our party on the other side.

"Lucky we get here today," Upa said.

My horse was trembling and so was I. My teeth chattered involuntarily. The blinding rain had not ceased. I didn't feel lucky.

"If we had waited another day, we would not be able to cross," he reminded me.

The thought of spending another night at his

uncle's helped cure me of any regret. The rain let up momentarily. I spied a rider descending the ridge overlooking Hakalau gulch. Kilani galloped to meet him. Her husband turned out to be a white man who arrived leading fresh mounts. Strangely, the presence of a white man calmed me. I was given a powerful gelding to make the rest of the journey to Hilo.

At long last we arrived at the home of Bishop Willis where a cup of hot tea and a lavish meal awaited followed by a steaming bath to sooth aching muscles.

The weeks ahead were filled with fast rides through the forests of Puna capped off with a healing soak in Ahalanui pond. Upa took me to Akaka falls, a spectacular cascade spilling over moss-laden rocks to a pond framed in ferns and orchids glistening in the sun. I wanted to know more of the lush hauntingly beautiful Islands. I ventured to Maui where I rode up the flank of Haleakala and descended inside the lunar landscape of the dormant volcano. I explored Iao Valley sheltered by steep pali where fierce battles were fought between the defending Mauins and the conquering warriors of Kamehameha I.

My health continued to improve in the nurturing clime of the Islands. I felt stronger and more vibrant than any time of my life. I was no longer a weakling suffering from headaches and melancholy. My back was strong. I could ride for hours without pain. I was tempted to stop my journey here in these lazy isles, but I feared an indolent life would set in. I would become content and lose all ambition. Like so many who have landed here by design or fate, I would forget where I came from and lose all desire to return. Having spent half of my life bedridden, I couldn't allow this to happen. I had to know the mysteries of the American West and venture on to lands yet unknown.

I returned to Hilo for one last respite before taking passage to San Francisco. Six days had turned into six months in the Sandwich Islands. On the way to the dock to board the Kilauea for the sail back to Honolulu, I asked Bishop Willis about Upa. He had disappeared. I wanted to thank him for leading me to the home of Pele, extending to me the warmth of his family, and giving me the courage to press on. But mostly, I wanted to see his boyish face slashed by an impish smile and the devil sparkling in his splendid eyes.

"I'm sorry, Isabella. He can't say goodbye. He contracted leprosy and was taken to Moloka'i where he will spend the rest of his life at Kalapaupau," Bishop Willis informed me.

This news saddened me to the core. Disease

brought to the Islands by foreigners has decimated the native populations. I knew of the notorious leper colony enclosed by 3,000-foot sea cliffs. Apparently, there was no escape path from the village hidden from sight. The vibrant, joyful Upa would never see his wife and young son again. He was to be imprisoned in his body isolated from his ohana, or extended family, for the rest of his days. He had helped me break the shackles of pain that once bound me, and now he was to know that sorrow. My thoughts went to the baleful look in Halemanu's eyes when he said, "Soon there will be no more kanakas."

Onward to Colorado

The passage from Honolulu to San Francisco aboard the Costa Rica was peaceful with agreeable passengers for company. Hours were spent playing chess, lounging on the deck gazing upon the expanse of blue stretching to eternity, and reading tales of high adventure in distant lands. I recalled my first blue water crossing on the Canada, a 300-foot paddle wheel steamer packed with 186 passengers. A chess tournament was proposed to fill the time. I had spent many happy hours playing chess with my grandfather, so I eagerly agreed to the challenge. The final match became a heated contest between me and a snow-capped elderly gentleman with a bushy mustache who was retired military. It took four hours to corner him into checkmate. My exultation was short-lived as the man's face flushed a bright red and he pushed away from the board in a heated display. He nearly knocked over his chair in his haste to leave the lounge.

Onlookers stared at me in disbelief. The women looked at me with accusatory expressions. Apparently, I was to let the gentleman win rather than forcing him to lose face. The men in the room turned their backs on me as I walked away.

Memories of treasured moments in Hawai'i and anticipation of my adventures to come in Colorado occupied my daydreams during this cruise. Miss Karpe's descriptions of the untamed Rocky Range filled me with a longing to know the lofty peaks. These days passed slowly giving my body time to recuperate from the strenuous rides through the gulches and valleys and peaks of Hawai'i. Could there be any more stunning vistas than there to be held close to my heart? It seemed impossible, yet the answer to that question propelled me forward.

San Francisco with its clanging ships bells, moaning harbor buoys, barking harbor seals, and pungent scent of the sea was a welcome feast of the senses. But gray mist hung in the air, sending a chill down my spine reminding me of why I left my homeland. I couldn't wait to get to the curative dry, thin air of Colorado. Invalids in the thousands suffering from consumption, asthma, and other nerve diseases flocked there for the camp cure. My maladies are not so specific, but the damp of England brings on feelings of despair and an ache in my bones. I wasted no time boarding a train for Cheyenne and leaving the dreary shroud of fog over San Francisco behind.

California truly is the land of milk and honey. As the train trundled through golden fields, I saw mounds of yellow squash, pudgy pumpkins, crimson tomatoes, cantaloupe, melons of all kinds, and corn in green husks resting on loading platforms waiting to be delivered. I envied passengers in the sleeping car that night as I spent it sitting up gazing into starless heavens. In late afternoon, the train began the ascent into the Sierras overlooking deep ravines carved by charging torrents. We entered miles-long tunnels called snow sheds that shut out all light. Cool temperatures greeted us in the rough town of Truckee where men stood around blazing fires drinking openly in public. The bar room in the only hotel was filled with boisterous men smoking and drinking to the clinking sounds of an out-of-tune piano.

I spent an uncomfortable night there. Next day, I engaged a horse I would soon wish I'd never met to take me to Lake Tahoe. The stable hand offered me a traditional ladies' side saddle, which I refused. The groom assured me, "You can do whatever you please here in Truckee."

I stood on a log stump to mount the fractious beast. My leg went halfway down his barrel. He strained to gallop, and I gave him his head for several miles to settle him down. It felt good to sink into his lumbering gait and feel secure in the deep seat of the western saddle. The track was pleasant enough plowed to dust by pack trains delivering goods to gold mines. Sunlight streamed through the towering pines and silver spruce. The intoxicating air laden with their scent livened my senses. Along the way I passed a freight wagon pulled by twenty-six oxen with a saddle horse tethered behind. The driver waved to me as I passed him by.

In my periphery I saw the shadow of a dark figure I thought was a wild boar in the understory. The horse knew otherwise; he reared and went into a tailspin. I was told these woods are filled with black and grizzly bears but that they don't attack if left alone. The horse didn't believe any of this and turned into a bucking bronco tossing me into the air. I had a soft landing in pine needles, but the horse with a lopsided saddle was sprinting out of sight. I was left with my tapestry bag and a wet horse pad. The shadow I assumed it was a bear, disappeared and I was left standing alone. I gathered my belonging and headed after the irascible animal. It looked to be a long walk back to Truckee.

As luck would have it, the teamster saw the

horse running wild and remembered the single lady he saw in passing. He had somehow retrieved the brute and brought him back to me, demonstrating the high regard even the roughest Westerner has for a lady. Reunited with my mount, I was able to press on to the singular lodging on the rim of Lake Tahoe. Such an enchanting sight. The sunset that night was unutterably beautiful with a full cast of colors to fill any artist's palette. Towering pines skirted the sapphire gem of a lake. God's handiwork unsurpassed was worth a few bruises. I returned to Truckee to catch the eastbound train to Cheyenne. I spent another night there where miners, loggers, cowboys, and outlaws of all stripes gather around blazing fires and raucousness prevails unchecked.

The clack, clack, clack of the train barreling across vast expenses of prairie became a lullaby. I was greeted by stifling summer heat when I stepped off the train in Cheyenne. Murders by stabbing and shooting are not uncommon in this uncivilized rim of the West. Wooden structures thrown together hastily serve as houses without gardens or ornament. Gangs of mangy dogs and men of unscrupulous character wander the dusty streets. I managed to hire a buggy driven by a sullen young man to deliver me to my lodging. After 45 jostling miles on a rutted track under an unforgiving sun, I arrived at the home of the Chalmers where I was told a cabin was available for rent.

Mrs. Chalmers, a hard, sad looking woman, met me at the door of a ramshackle house.

"The side cabin's not been kept up. It has holes in the roof and is infested with vermin. Haven't rented it for years, but you can share a bed with my daughter for eight dollars a week, if you can make yourself agreeable," she said.

I looked beyond her to see her daughter, a repellant looking creature, wearing a drab brown dress with tawny hair that had not seen a comb in days. I could not go back to Cheyenne, and it was too far to get to Longmont, my next stop. Life here was rougher than anywhere I have seen, but I chose to make myself "agreeable."

The heat and flies in the house were so unbearable the entire family moved outdoors at night. Beds of pine boughs covered with tattered sheets became our sleeping mats. Drifting to sleep beneath a velvet sky with a swath of stars with this God-forsaken, God-forgotten family was much preferable to sleeping indoors. People can safely sleep outdoors here six months of the year. The rainfall on the plains of Colorado is far below average, the air rarified, dews are rare, and fog unknown. The din of grasshoppers, flies, and locusts along with the night chorus of coyotes, wolves, and hoot owls was un-nerving. I killed a rattlesnake that was close to the cabin and found it had eleven joints in its rattle. Rattlesnakes abound here along with moccasin snakes, carpet snakes, and green racers.

Mrs. Chalmers washed graying garments on a stone with lye then hung them to flap in the ceaseless dry wind. The daughter was given the duty of slopping the hogs in a makeshift piggery. They snorted and grunted with satisfaction at the tubers she gathered for them. Mr. Chalmers milked two pitiful looking cows that gave very little milk. Tough, greasy, fly-blown meat, and biscuits was our fare for breakfast, lunch, and dinner. I made myself further agreeable by washing dishes, sweeping floors, and offering to mend tattered clothing.

I spoke to Mr. Chalmers of my desire to get to Estes Parks as soon as possible. He arrived here as a consumptive two years ago and had seen the camp cure. But the price of health was dear for him and his family eking out a mere existence. He was not a good farmer and not much good at anything else, according to Mrs. Chalmers. However, he claimed to know the way to Estes Park and said he could provide me a mount. Anxious to get on to my destination I agreed to let him be my guide. Mrs.

Chalmers hadn't left the endless labors of her hopeless life in years, so she asked if she could join us. She put together food supplies she called "grub" to last the several days journey.

Mr. Chalmers appeared the next morning with a sorry excuse for a horse that would be my mount. The poor fellow was an iron grey, bony beast with a lip hung down exposing yellow teeth. He barely had energy to swat the swarming flies with his scruff of a tail. It would be a kindness to take him to pasture and let him live out his days there. I wore my flannel Hawaiian riding dress with a handkerchief tied over my face to protect me from the dust and unrelenting sun. My bridle consisted of one rotten strand of leather and a frayed rope on the other side of a battered halter. I tucked an umbrella in my saddle bag to add more shelter to the ride. Mrs. Chalmers rode astride another broken-down nag. A pot and a bag of clothes hung from her saddle horn with layers of quilts behind. Mr. Chalmers, with cook pots dangling from his saddle and mismatched boots, looked more like a tinker than a guide aboard his gaunt mule. It was a sorry expedition to behold.

Six hours on a snaking trail ascending to a plateau brought us to a vista point overlooking Estes Park far below framed in defiant spires. A deep chasm carved through tinctured rock by the

Big Thompson River lie between us and our destination.

"The scenery here is glorious combining grace with sublimity," I said trying to hold my excitement in check. "This is true wildness—the realm of the beasts!"

Mr. Chalmer's merely grunted and pointed to the tallest peak without a hint of humanity between me and the mountains.

"That would be Longs Peak," he said.

Towering over Estes Park, Longs Peak is the tallest of many over 14,000-foot peaks in the Front Range of the Rockies. Miss Karpe told me that few have been able to reach the summit, but those that have find it a singularly uplifting experience. A powder white cape of snow on the shoulders of the monarch glistened in the afternoon sun. Dazzling like diamonds, it fired my desire to know the world from the peak's lofty vantage; to stand above the clouds and see to eternity at the seat of God. Now, I was even more determined to get to Estes Park, and on to the upper world.

Chalmers nonchalantly broke into a hunter's cabin where we proceeded to have lunch. After finishing our portion of beef jerky and tea, we began a descent that Mr. C said would take us down to the Big Thompson. We would have to cross this mighty river and the precipitous canyon it had carved to reach Estes Park. We began by navigating rocky dry streambeds and fields of cacti. Gulches too precarious to enter forced us to backtrack and find another way to conquer the steep terrain. The trail we were on now was nothing more than an animal track leading to nowhere. My horse was the first to slip on an angled sheet of rock and fall, rolling over landing against a stump. I had jumped off before being crushed, but not without being torn and bruised by jagged rocks on landing. My horse managed to right itself. As I was struggling to hand walk it back up the incline, Mrs. C's horse lost footing and rolled down the hill taking the poor women with it. The girth on her saddle, frayed when we started, gave way on the fall. She was badly shaken, but no bones were broken. She sat there crying for her fall, but more bitterly so knowing her husband was hopelessly lost. We salvaged the girth with Mr. Chalmers' belt and Mrs. C reluctantly remounted her frazzled horse.

Chalmers admitted he'd made a wrong turn, but insisted he knew the way out of our conundrum. We gathered ourselves and followed him up what turned out to be a climb in the wrong direction. He made a boisterous attempt at merriment to distract us from our misery. By now, we had run out of water, food, and good humor. I have a keen sense of direction. I knew we were headed the wrong way. After several hours of meandering, I intervened.

"I'm afraid I must commandeer from here, Mr. Chalmers," I dared say to this braggart who would not admit to his grotesque failure.

"I'm going with Ms. Bird," Mrs. Chalmer's declared.

I was much surprised at her brave defiance of her husband, but she knew his charade was turning deadly. I took the lead and after two hours of backtracking found our trail to the Chalmers' homestead. I pressed my mount into a brisk trot. While Mrs. C was struggling to keep up, the girth on of her weathered saddle came loose again and the saddle slipped off to the side taking the hapless woman with it. She hit the ground hard. With this latest calamity, I determined we should lead our fatigued mounts the last four miles to give them a respite before they collapsed beneath us. Mrs. C was only too glad to be on foot. We reached the homestead well after dark with frost in the air. I slept once again beneath velvet skies dreaming of knowing the upper world and the mysteries of Longs Peak.

Chalmers arranged another horse for my journey to Longmont where he assured me the St. Vrain Trail would take me to the inner world of the

Rockies. This horse was a half-broke, skittish mare. No sooner did I step into the stirrup did she begin to whirl about. Once I was seated, she took the bit and charged into the field where she jumped a log in her path sending me flying off her backside. A solid kick to my knee was her parting favor. No bones were broken, but the knee swelled to the size of a purple eggplant. Badly bruised, I was unable to ride. I managed to catch a lift with a passing delivery wagon going to Longmont where I hoped to find lodging at the St. Vrain Hotel owned by the Bakers. I was pleased to leave these dreary people and their grinding life behind.

After an exhausting journey beneath a fierce sun across the plains, we entered Longmont. Converging wagon tracks led to a wide straggling street with frame houses and a few shops with wooden fronts. A two-story white house on the banks of the St. Vrain River, the social hub of the town, was to be my hotel. There I was greeted by Mr. and Mrs. Baker, congenial hosts who wished to see to my every comfort.

"Miss Bird we are so flattered to have you in our company," said Mr. Baker, a kindly gentleman in black pants, vest, and crisp white shirt who eagerly took my bag and ushered me into the sitting room. "Miss Karpe sent a letter letting us know you might be stopping by."

"Would you give us the pleasure of joining us for tea?" said Mrs. Baker, a plump woman with pink cheeks and gray wisps of hair pulled into a tidy topknot.

"What a relief to be in civilized society once again," I said to Mrs. Baker as she ushered in warm scones with creamy butter and tea on a serving tray.

"We understand you wish to venture to Estes Park," she said.

"Yes. How did you know?" I was not aware of any announcements.

"Your reputation for adventure proceeds you," Mr. Baker said, pulling out a newspaper clipping and handing it me.

A Scotch lassie named Miss Bird, all the way from "Edinburgh Town," literary in tastes, adventurous in travel, and withal an invalid in health, is now in this Territory, en route round the world, from the west. From Australia to Hawai'i to California, by steamer; across the State of California on horseback to Nevada, at the rate of forty miles a day, she is now ready and willing to ride up and through our Rocky Mountains, for the fun of it. Rocky Mountain Herald Sept 13, 1873

It seems Miss Karpe informed the local newspapers of my arrival in this fair region. I wished she hadn't pressed about my horsemanship.

I felt in quite a feeble state after my exploratory with the Chalmers. I was not certain I could make the thirty-mile ride from the hotel to Estes Park. My back was not troubling me, but my knee was still quite swollen.

"All that is true, except I favored the train over horseback to Cheyenne. It is my deepest desire to reach the summit of Longs Peak before moving on," I said.

"I wish you could enjoy a good rest here, but the season for entering the park is fast coming to a close. If you want go to Estes, you will have to go soon. September can be this most stunning time of year there, but you risk the chance of being snowed in for the winter!" Mr. Baker feared I could be making a mistake.

"I have seen the wonders from afar. I will regret not being able to know them closer, but I will leave for Denver and on to New York in the morning if there is no chance of my obtaining a guide to Estes Park," I said, trying to be reasonable.

"Aye, it would be a real shame to miss the most beautiful scenery in Colorado on your tour," he said.

Mrs. Baker chimed in, "There is only one man who guides tourists up Longs Peak and he can be quite disagreeable."

"Now, Mary, that's not fair, Jim has always

done well by us. He brought us that roast you are fixing tonight."

"That's true, but he is given to drunken rages and is quite unpredictable. I am afraid Miss Bird will not be in the most careful hands."

"Who might this gentleman be by name?" I wanted to know who to ask for when I arrived, so as not to waste any more time.

"He is James Nugent, but he goes by Rocky Mountain Jim. Nobody really knows where he came from, but you have to cross his land to get to Evans place. Word has it he's handy with a pistol and has used it on visitors when he is in one of his fits."

"Now Mary, that's all talk. You don't need to frighten Miss Bird."

I excused myself and went to my room that was swarming with flies and tried to rest in the oppressive heat. I was feeling most downhearted regretting the wasted time with the Chalmers. It could mean that I will not reach my goal after traveling all these miles. Now, if I was lucky, I would have to contend with a madman for my guide. A timid knock stirred me from my fretful nap.

"Are you able to ride at a lope? Are you afraid of the cold? Can you "rough it?" Mr. Baker peppered me with these and more questions.

I assured him I could though my honest answer would have been, *I hope so*.

"Then you are in luck!" he exclaimed.

The hotel is the gathering place for single men in search of a home-cooked meal. Two of what Mr. Baker termed "innocent men" for which I was not sure of his meaning were leaving in the morning for the park. They were hunters who knew the trail who said they would take me for a fee.

"Really? The Lord has answered my prayers!"

"Indeed, he has, but I'm not sure you will be pleased with the result," Mr. Baker chuckled.

"They will take you as far as the Evans Lodge where you can find comfort. I will arrange a horse for you. Be ready by eight in the morning to ride."

I hoped the accommodation at Evans Lodge would not be as rough as the Chalmers and feared that solitude would be impossible, but I was ready to pay the price. I lay awake all night in a state of eager anticipation.

The two young men, Jake and Gabe, eyed me suspiciously when they saw me in my flannel Hawaiian riding dress and Turkish pantaloons. Gabe was tall and lanky with a red kerchief around his tanned neck. He wore leather breaches and a fringed, rawhide jacket. The tail of a raccoon dangled from his fur cap. Jake was stocky with a three-day beard wearing denim jeans and plaid shirt. They both holstered pistols on their hips and rifles in their scabbards. They feared they had made a grave mistake to take an odd woman "known to be invalid" into the mountains. Like sailors setting out on a sea voyage, they exchanged glances that told me they thought taking a woman was going to be bad luck. I paid them a princely sum to be my guides and hoped their reluctance to take me would not be rewarded.

My mount was no less hesitant sizing me up with restless ears and rolling eyes. She was a high-spirited, beautiful creature with arched neck and quivering nostrils. The mare looked to be part Arab with a dish face and sleek conformation not fit to carry gear. Still, I slung my pack behind the Mexican saddle that seemed too heavy for her and my canvas bag with clothing on the horn. It took both men to hold her steady while I mounted. She pranced eager to get on with it.

The sky was a cloudless, deep brilliant blue. Though the sun was hot, the morning air was fresh and bracing. We galloped across plains for the first six miles or so at an exhilarating pace. My horse proved to be perfection. Fresh and energetic she needed no prompting. I settled into the deep seat of the saddle and relaxed into her floating stride. Her movements were graceful, effortless, and solid. When we entered the canyon carved by the St. Vrain River, she was sure-footed as any Hawaiian pony clomping through the streams without hesitation. The slightest touch of leg brought immediate reward. It was heaven to be on a horse trained by voice and gentle commands rather than the stick and draconian bits. I felt I could ride a hundred miles as easily as thirty on this mare with legs of iron. I named her Birdie and determined to keep her for my entire mountain tour.

As we got closer, we entered the gloom of the chasm carved by the river. Sheer rock walls veined in a palette of burnt orange, vermillion, and yellow with traces of turquoise colored the scene. It was a devious trail following the many twists and turns of the river requiring many crossings. I could only hope the "innocent men" would not lose their bearings. The canyon opened to a river corridor lined in trembling yellow aspen leaves spinning like gold medallions in the brisk wind. Scarlet vines of poison oak carpeted the riverbanks and wound around the trunks of trees. At length, we began to climb out of the canyon into the blue shadows of the pitch pine forest.

We left the tracks of humankind and plunged into the wilds of the Rocky Mountains. Here is the land of the beasts: the giant grizzly bear, the sneaking mountain lion, and majestic elk share the mountains with the lesser creatures. All reside in balance and harmony with territories neatly staked out by scent. Elation mounted with the fantastic views that revealed themselves around each bend in the climb. Below vast meadows, beyond austere granite peaks, above heaven's blue dome. I was overtaken with a sense of aloneness—not in a frightening way, but in a sacred way. I had entered the "Great Alone" where man has not made his mark. Tender vulnerability and an overwhelming sense of privilege brought tears to my eyes. We crested a plateau from which I could see snow-streaked Longs Peak in the distance. I was reeling in reverie when Gabe held up his hand signaling us to stop.

"This is as far as we go Miss Bird," he said.

"What!" I was a bit shaken at this news.

"You are going to the Evans place. It's about four miles over yonder," he said pointing in a north-easterly direction. "It's about a half mile to Muggin's Gulch where you will likely meet up with Rocky Mountain Jim. He thinks he is the gate keeper of the Rocky Range. He can tell you how to get to Evans Lodge from his place."

"What about you?" I was worried about how I would return to Longmont.

"We are going to do a little huntin' and fishin' ma'am. You will find other borders at Evans place."

"Thank you for bringing me this far," I said.

Gabe tipped his hat and spurred his horse on.

As they trotted off, I felt both relieved and frightened at the loss of their less-than-congenial company. Eagerly anticipating my arrival to the inner world, I turned Birdie towards Evans Lodge.

My Name is James Nugent

Colorado, 1863
Ten Years Earlier

My Name is James Nugent – Rocky Mountain Jim

Running Deer and I crawled on our bellies to a knoll overlooking a meadow where a herd of elk grazed in knee-high grass. We wore our wolf caps with ears to fool the elk if they saw us. There was a headwind blowing up canyon, so they didn't pick up our scent. We decided to go for a bull with a full rack. He was thickly muscled in his prime, real regal lookin'. He would be enough to feed the entire village. We slithered silently on the ground to get a closer shot. Running Deer could bring him down with his bow and arrow, but I had my rifle at the ready in case he missed. We didn't want any other hunters, Indian, or otherwise, who might be in ear shot to hear the crack of a rifle. In one swift move Running Deer stood, pulled an arrow from his quiver, took aim, and let his arrow fly. It stuck home. The animal lifted his head to see his enemy and stared at us with a questioning, intelligent eye. I let loose with my rifle and got him in the chest. This brought him to his knees. The rest of the herd thundered away. Excited at our kill, we ran down the slope to make certain he was dead.

"You got him good," I said.

"Should have hit him in the chest," Running Deer said, as he pulled his arrow from the neck of the elk.

"No matter, you got 'em."

"He's too big to carry," Running Deer said.

We had left our horses hobbled in a meadow about a half mile away. "I'll stay here and you can go get the horses, break down camp, and bring our outfit to me. Let's hang him up and bleed him out on that tree yonder before you go."

We tied the elk with rope around its rear legs, threw the rope over the limb of the tree. Then we took hold of the rope and hauled him up. We skinned the fur around his hooves and slit arteries so he would drain and not be too heavy to carry out.

Running Deer got to the horses and brought back our gear.

"Go back to the village and get a travois so we can haul him out of here," I told him. "I will stay here and keep the wolves at bay."

Estes Park has long been the summer hunting grounds of the Cheyenne. Chief Black Kettle's village of about 130 teepees followed the game. Running Deer was part of his tribe camped on the bank of the Big Thompson River. I met Running Deer at the missionary school in Denver. I was thirteen at the time and he was a bit older. Indian kids and settler kids both attended the missionary school overseen by my father, a Presbyterian preacher. Running Deer was sent to the school by his tribe to learn how to read, write, and speak English, so he could translate for the chiefs during their talks with the whites. He bunked at the missionary orphanage during the school term.

When I turned sixteen, I got to go with Running Deer to where his village was camped in the Rockies. When school let out for the summer, we would head for the Front Range where we set traps and did some huntin' and fishin'. I learned the ways of his tribe. My father didn't like me running with an Indian, but he was happy to see the game I brought home. Running Deer taught me how to trap beavers, mink, and otters. He was an excellent tracker and we never missed getting game when we went out. We were free trappers and sold our pelts to the highest bidder. Sometimes we traded them for tack and supplies so we could spend summers hunting and fishing in the mountains camped out beneath a swath of stars.

Book learning in the winter was fine, but I

lived for summers tramping over the mountains to glacier tarns beneath craggy peaks streaked with snow. The meadows were flush with wildflowers: lupine, larkspur, and columbine. Bluebirds, orange orioles, and yellow tanagers flitted among the spinning aspen leaves. It was always great to get an elk, a deer, or maybe an antelope, but it never really mattered to me. I just loved being free in the mountains. It always kinda hurt me to kill a beautiful creature, but Running Deer told me it was all part of the eternal circle of life.

Running Deer would have to go about 20 miles out and 20 miles back with the travois. The night turned crystalline with the stars crackling in the heavens and nearly a full moon. I could see my breath, so I lay close to the fire using my saddle for a pillow. I was slipping into dreamland when I heard my horse hobbled nearby let out a high-pitched whinny that spoke of danger. I pulled on my boots and grabbed my rifle. It could be hostile Indians, or just some critter looking for a free meal. Then, I saw him! A monster grizzly standing at least twelve feet tall stretched up to reach the carcass of the elk. He clawed at the elk with paws big as frying pans. At first, I froze, but then I made the mistake of letting him know I was there.

"Git bear!" I yelled.

I fired letting a bullet whiz by his head. I

didn't want to wound him; that would just make him mad. I was hoping to scare him off. Instead of running away, he turned towards me. His orange eyes glittered like fire, and he stood on his hind legs, pawed the air, and puffed up the back of his neck. He let out a ferocious growl and starting woofing. He was aiming to attack. My gun would not kill him if he got serious. I stood stalk still knowing that if I ran it would become a cat and mouse game I would lose. I tried not to stare at him because I knew that would be a challenge to him. Saliva dripped from his canines as he let out a horrifying roar and charged.

Sometimes, these critters are just bluffing, but this guy wasn't. He came straight for me. I fired. The bullet reached its mark but didn't slow him. He tore the rifle from me with one swipe, dislocating my shoulder. He sunk his fangs into my stomach, lifted me up and shook me like a rag doll then dropped me to the ground. I was reeling from the blow when he placed his great jaws around the top of my head. His hot breath was rank. His tongue wet. I could hear the bones crunching in my skull as he pressed down with massive canines. His saliva mixed with my blood blinded me. He didn't release my head from his powerful jaws. I managed to get my skinning knife out of its sheath and stabbed it wildly until it found purchase and sunk into what I thought might be his eye. He loosened his hold on me long enough to let out another savage growl then spun around tearing off what felt like half my face and most of my scalp with a parting swipe of his paw.

I blacked out. When I came to, the world was spinning. I made out through blurred vision that the bear was still trying to pull the elk down from the tree. When it fell to the ground, he turned around and started in my direction. I knew to play dead. That was my only hope. If he decided to chaw on me again, I would be a goner. He came over snuff-ling around my body sniffing for signs of life. I held my breath and prayed he didn't have a taste for humans. Satisfied his work was done, he turned and shambled off dragging our kill with him.

I laid there wondering if I was going to bleed out. I could only see out of my left eye. I couldn't lift my right arm; it lay limp. I was too weak to raise my left arm to feel the damage to my face. I think my ribs were cracked or maybe even broken. A shaft of white lightning went through me if I tried to move. I prayed Running Deer would get to me soon.

My next memory was his voice fading in and out, and the agony of him trying to manipulate my body. "I should never have left you," I heard Running Deer say. His voice sounded far away like in a dream. "Hold on brother, I will get you back to my village," he said.

It was a slow arduous return to the village on the travois. I floated in and out of consciousness with many jolts sending pain ripping through my body. When I awoke in his teepee sometime later, I would understand that he had cleaned me up as best he could. He had cut a blanket in strips and wrapped my wounds and had restored my eyeball back in the socket and wrapped a bandana around my head to keep it in place.

A pot of steaming water hung from a tripod of sticks over the flickering fire in the center of the teepee. I lay on a bear skin rug covered in a blanket. My vision was blurred, but I could make out the form of a woman kneeling beside me.

"Don't move," she said. "I will be careful, but I need to clean your wounds. You are lucky Running Deer could bring you to us in time. You are in Black Kettle's village. You were very close to death, but the Great Spirit is not ready for you. I will try not to hurt you, but I must remove your clothes." She soothed me with her gentle voice as she and Running Deer lifted my limbs and cut my shirt and pants stiff with blood from my body.

Shining Moon cleansed my wounds with a warm cloth. Her round, soft face was framed in ink black hair that went to her waist. She wore a dress, leggings and moccasins made of deerskin and a headband decorated with beads. I reckon she was the most beautiful woman I ever saw. Her warm breath and sweet smile comforted me as she placed a poultice of crushed yarrow leaves on my face. Before leaving me, she placed a cooling wet deerskin over my eye socket.

Running Deer's squaw, Shining Moon, is the daughter of White Snake a powerful medicine man. I was to receive her tender mercies until I could return to my father's house in Denver. The Cheyenne are nomads living light on the land. Wonderful horsemen, they follow the great herds of buffalo and take the shaggy beasts down with well-placed arrows. Masterful craftsman and strong warriors, I learned many lessons from them.

I was not to touch my face while it was healing, but I feared the truth awaiting me. I am not a vain man, but was graced with an appearance the ladies liked. I inherited my father's piercing blue eyes, flaxen hair, and sturdy Scandinavian build. My father worked fourteen-hour days tending to his parish in Denver and minding our homestead. He read from the Bible at breakfast, lunch, and dinner. He held services every Sunday at his church and rode to the settlers' homes on the plains around Denver providing solace to the ill. I tended our crops, corn for our milk cows, and ma's vegetable garden. The pig pen and horse stalls always needed cleaning and I chopped enough wood to keep us good all winter. My father believed a person needed work to keep him from Satan's temptations.

My mother labored as many hours a day cooking, cleaning, and mending, but found respite from the day's tedium in her books. When I was a child, she read to me each evening about a world outside I could only imagine before drifting off to sleep. My father only read from the Good Book. He stopped me from reading what he considered to be frivolous escapism when I was old enough to help him tend to the endless chores. When I turned eighteen, he planned to have me enlist in the Union Army to fight the war raging in the South. But I had other plans.

Hunting and trapping trips with Running Deer were all I cared about. An accomplished hunter, he taught me how to lay traps for beavers and how to stretch the pelts to dry. We lay traps in the streams stealing through the meadows in the spring and collected our bounty to sell at the trading posts. He rode bareback with a light bit on one strand of leather. Like a centaur, he became a part of his horse. He carried his arrows in a quiver made from a mountain lion's leg. He could hit a mark with his bow and arrow at a full gallop. This was what was needed when hunting buffalo. His people used the buffalo hides for the walls of their teepees, clothing, and food. They traveled to the plains each year where the vast herds graze.

As I lay in the dark wondering if I would ever regain full vision, and what I would look like when my face healed, the scent of meat cooking slowly over coals stirred my appetite. I heard the voices of laughing children running around the camp, barking dogs, and the chatter of the women preparing the evening meal. Shining Moon appeared with a blackberry tea she had prepared that would help me fight off infections, and a bowl of broth.

"You cannot chew yet," she said as she helped the liquids to my mouth. I longed for a piece of the succulent meat scenting the air, but just the thought of chewing was painful.

"My father is coming to help you," she said, then vanished.

The teepee flap opened, and White Snake entered. His weathered faced was painted with white streaks. He wore an elaborate headdress of eagle feathers with dangling strands of ermine skins.

He didn't speak as he floated a feather in his gnarled brown hand the entire length of my body trying to sense the inner damage. My arm was limp and useless by my side. If I moved even slightly, a shaft of pain that seemed to originate in my ribs shot through my whole body. My face felt numb. He lifted my arm, placed his moccasin foot beneath my armpit, and gave a mighty tug on my arm shifting the joint back into place. I cried out in agony.

"What the bejesus are you doing to me?" My shoulder was on fire.

He didn't say anything and put his finger to his lips indicating I should be quiet. He lifted a round drum over my mid-section, beating it slowly as he doused my body to release tension and rebalance my energies. He chanted while he drummed. After his examination and treatment, he took out three eagle feathers from his medicine pouch and wafted them over the length of my body as he continued to chant. He handed Shining Moon a pouch and left as quietly as he had entered.

"What did he say?" I asked Shining Moon.

"Earth Mother take this white back into your womb. Let him be reborn. Let him do the Earth Walk in harmony with you. Give him Grandfather Sun's warm breath and Grandmother Moon to rest."

"You are to drink this powder from hops flowers with water. I will prepare some for you now; it will make you sleep," she said.

I wanted to believe his medicine would help me. I drank the mixture and soon drifted off.

The People

I lost count of how long I was in Running Deer's teepee before I dared to try to stand. Running Deer helped me up and led me out to the fire where the men were smoking their pipe and sharing stories. Smoke drifted lazily to the glittering heavens. Strips of meat hanging on drying racks beneath smoking fires spoke of a successful buffalo hunt. The hoot of owls talking to one another of the night's catch and the howl of wolves were the evening's chorus. I couldn't understand the men as they passed the pipe, snorted, and laughed, but I guessed they talked about the bravery displayed in the hunt. It didn't matter. It was the warmth of the fire and human companionship that was earth medicine for me.

One night, Shining Moon led me to a teepee where an elder was talking to the people. Children of all ages and their mothers sat cross-legged in a circle around the old chief. A blazing fire before him cast a glow upon their faces as they clustered around him. They stared with wonder as the proud warrior withered with time told them of their beginnings. His deeply set eyes sparkled with inner amusement. “The Great Mystery placed the Eternal Flame of Love in the center of every living thing. This flame is the connection that makes us all family and the glue that holds Creation together,” he said as he gazed upon the children.

“The animals are all part of Creation and we have much to learn from them. We two-leggeds have fewer powers than many of Earth Mother’s creations. The Eagle brings messages from the Creator to the hawk who has the power of vision and can fly and observe from many different angles. He gives his message to the crow who in turn gives it to The People.

“Each of the creatures has something to teach us. Wolves have a strict order of duty and are a close family unit. They show us how to live together with respect and harmony.”

The children listened intently as he continued with his talk of how the animals each impart a lesson to us if we are listening.

“The snake is a creature of renewal. He sheds his skin making way for a better life. Even though change can be painful, it brings a better future. We are in a time of great change and we must bend or be broken. We must shed our old ways and learn how to follow the path the Great Mystery has laid out for us. The deer is a shy creature whose presence calms us. That is why I have chosen Running Deer to learn how to talk to the whites for us."

At that moment, I realized this was the great peace chief Black Kettle himself. He was trying to help his people understand that their world was changing and that they had to adapt. The warriors of the tribe were not there. They were on a hunt. He chose this time to mold the minds of the children—the future of The People.

Two moons passed before I felt well enough to return to my own people. My ribs were tender, but I could sit a horse. My right arm was pretty much useless, but better. I could lift it a few inches and work my fingers. The right eye did not recover sight. My face, well, that would never be the same. I went to the creek and dared a look at my rippled reflection. The entire right side of my face was disfigured. It caved in beneath the cheek bone and a flap of flesh fell over my right eye socket. A jagged scar ran from my forehead to my chin. Tears glistened in the eye of the stranger staring back at me. A well of pity was filling from an underground spring no one would ever be allowed to see.

Shining Moon made a patch for my eye to

cover the dangling lid. I would have to learn to hunt with my rifle on my left shoulder, but I was alive. It was high time for me to return to my family in Denver. I'm sure Ma was worried, and Pa would be fuming because I wasn't there to help. A hint of fall was in the air. Winter comes quick in the mountains. I needed to get back to Denver to help my family prepare before the snow flies. Black Kettle's village would be breaking camp and heading down to the plains soon. It was time to move on.

"We will make a sweat for you," Running Deer said.

As a parting gift he wanted me to have a cleansing ceremony. He knew my thoughts were heavy and that I would need courage to re-enter my old world. Willows that bend with grace and don't break easily formed a curved rib structure covered with buffalo hide. Rocks placed in a fire pit in the center of the sweat lodge were heated until they glowed red. The hot rocks were then sprinkled with sacred water creating a steaming mist scented with burning cedar wood.

Before I was allowed to enter, Running Deer waved a smudge stick made of herbs woven with sage over me. He tapped it on the top of my head and shoulders. This was to begin the cleansing process.

"Get on your knees and take off your boots," he instructed. "The entrance to the lodge is low to the ground to remind us to be humble."

I crawled on hands and knees through the narrow entrance to find six squaws facing six warriors sitting cross-legged in a circle around the steaming rocks. White Snake was sitting at the entrance and would guide the ceremony. He directed me to sit in the center of the semi-circle around the fire between the men and women.

He tapped his drum and gave a slow chant before speaking to us.

"We two-leggeds gather rust on our spirits. It grows into resentment, jealousy, envy, greed, and even hatred if we don't clear our thoughts of these feelings."

He tapped his drum again, sprinkled the rocks with sacred water filling the dome with steam.

The group responded by chanting "Ho" in unison.

"To know the power of fire, any sorrow or burden must be left outside of the circle of warmth."

Once again, the people replied "Ho."

This went on for several rounds. By then, I was sweating profusely. Water dribbled off my nose. White Snake must have noticed because his next words seem to be directed to me.

"Our sweat will nourish our mother. Water is

the source of all life. Water nurtures. It is not worn out as the earth. It is the blood flowing in the veins of our Earth Mother who is in need of our love."

More drumming, chanting, and a resounding "HO" from the circle gathered there to embrace me with cleansing energy.

I felt woozy. I heard my own voice saying. "I am a stranger here, but I believe there is a reason I have come to this place. I am lonely among my own kind."

The shaman responded. Tapping his drum and sprinkling more water upon the rocks, he said, "He has found The People. Give him your thoughts to help him find his courage."

"Ho," the Indians chanted, bestowing me with new strength to move on.

Betrayal

My mother's knees buckled when she saw my face. I reached out, breaking her fall and steadying her before she slumped to the kitchen floor.

"It's okay Ma, I'm alive."

"What happened to you?" she asked, holding back tears. She reached for my blonde locks she loved so well and slid them away from my face to see the full extent of the damage.

"I got caught out with a bear. It was my own stupid fault," I said.

My father stormed into the room. "Where you been? You have been gone all summer while I been…". He stopped mid-sentence at the sight of me. After a moment, he blurted out in anger, "I told you no good was going to come from you running with Indians."

"I wouldn't be **here** if Running Deer hadn't saved me."

"You wouldn't have been **there** if you had listened to me. You will enlist like your brother," he growled.

My brother Zeke, two years older than me, had joined the Union to fight the Confederates. He left a year ago and we had not heard anything from him since. Ma was beside herself with worry over him. I was the second in a line of ten children my mother had birthed. Two of them died before the age of one, the rest were still clinging to her apron strings. She cooked, cleaned, mended, and sewed clothes for all of them. At the age of forty she had a careworn expression and was bent over like an old woman. Her hands were red and flaked from the lye in the soap she used for scrubbing. She understood that I was different from my brother, that I had no stomach for war, but Father wouldn't hear it.

"While you were camped out with the Indians, there was a murderous attack on the Hungate family. They used Nathan's body for target practice. He had eighty bullet holes in him. His wife and two daughters were scalped, and their bodies were mutilated by your friends. Their bodies were paraded through Denver to let people know what's in store for them if we don't' retaliate."

"That wasn't Black Kettle's people. It must have been the Dog Soldiers," I said.

The Dog Soldiers are a militant band of rebels made up of different tribes who were not willing to let the whites take away the lands promised to them. They are merciless and determined to turn back the endless stream of wagon trains carrying settlers into their land. Treaties were made giving them land where game was plentiful, but they were quickly broken when gold was discovered in the Rockies and land was taken away once more.

"I don't care what name you give them. Indians have surrounded Denver and are cutting off supplies. The city is starving. People are scared. You have to take a side and it better be the side of your family or you aren't welcome in my house," he said.

My mother, powerless against my father, looked down at her feet and said nothing to change his mind.

"I'll be back to collect my things when I know where I'm going," I said. I wasn't sure where I would go, but I knew life with my family was over.

I went to the military headquarters in Denver. I didn't want to enlist, but I needed to do something. I entered the office of the recruiter, hat in hand and wearing my eye-patch.

"My name is Jim Nugent, sir. I'm looking to help the cause by feeding your men."

The recruiting officer took one look at my face and said, "You don't look fit to be a soldier."

"Can't argue with that sir, but I am a hunter. I know these mountains. I would like to join up with your trappers to get food for the troops."

"Alright Nugent, you can bunk with the other trappers in Estes Park. The army pays $250 a month. You get a mule to pack in the meat and provisions for the summer.

"Sounds good sir, thank you." It was a stroke of good luck to be assigned to quarters in the Front Range. Before heading out I went back to the house to gather up my belongings that included a dog-eared copy of *Moby Dick*. Fortunately, my father was not there. Ma hugged me and wished me well. I knew she was as glad as me that I was not going to war.

The rough-hewn log cabin the trappers used was nestled in a shady glen overlooking Lily Lake. It happened to be one of my favorite spots to lay traps for beaver, mink, and ermine with Running Deer. Two men, one cleaning tack and the other mucking the horses, stopped their labors to say hello.

"Howdy. What's your business here?" the taller of the two men asked.

"I come to help you hunt game for the cavalry," I said extending a friendly hand which was swallowed in his bear-like paw.

"I'm Billy Jo, and this here is my little brother Jody."

Billy Jo's little brother was about 250 pounds of muscle. His wore a flannel shirt, bandana around his thick neck, and a black felt hat. He hung back leaning on the rake he was using to clean the make-shift horse corral while Billy did the talking. Billy Jo needed a shave and haircut. Every bit a grizzled mountain man wearing buckskin pants and shirt. He even smelled the part.

"You look like you had a spat with a bear and lost," Billy Jo said. Jody snickered at this observation.

"Yea, all the good I can say about that is that I'm here to tell."

"Can happen to the best of us out there. You know those critters are damn unpredictable. We plan on getting an early start in the morning. Do you think you'll be coming along?"

"Sure. You got plenty of traps? I can set some here today and collect our catch when we get back."

"Those critters aren't good eating and the military ain't payin' us for them."

"We can sell 'em at the trading post and pick up some extra cash while we are out."

"Don't see no harm in that," Billy Jo said, spitting a glob of chewing tobacco to the side, then grinning with yellow teeth.

"Your mule is named Hardtack. Your responsibility is to see he's groomed and fed. He's picketed in the meadow yonder.

"Thanks. I'll go make his acquaintance."

We headed out next morning for the tall grass meadows hoping to find elk but didn't see any. I was happy just to be back in the high country. A cooling breeze off a silver stream snaking through meadow made me smile inside. I felt like I was home. While Hardtack grazed, I took a snooze on a rock in the sun.

"We set up camp next to a glacier tarn figuring to get an early start in the morning. Billy Jo gathered three sturdy sticks to form a tripod over the fire so we could hang our camp kettle to boil water for coffee. Buffalo jerky and potatoes heated in the coals made a fine dinner. Fur trappers are usually genial bunch who like to chaw around the fire, so I opened the floor to conversation.

"So where are you boys from?" I asked.

"We was trapping for a fur company in the headwaters of the Salmon River. The good Lord never made more bountiful country. Beavers were just one of the critters we bagged every time we went out. Deer, elk, mountain sheep and goats all are there for the takin'," Billy Jo said.

"So, why did you leave?"

"Wasn't our idea. Got swarmed by Blackfeet. We was just sitting down to a buffalo steak sizzling on the rocks by the fire when about sixty of them varmints come thundering down on us whooping and yelling like demons. Our horses were already out to graze and we was caught off guard. I grabbed my Hawkeye but didn't have time to fire. There were a baker's dozen of us and we all ran for cover. Jody and I ducked into the willows in the creek we camped by. We lay face down in the mud just under the water where they couldn't see us breathing through a reed. Volleys of arrows was whizzin' all around us. I heard the crack of a rifle. Lifted my head long enough to see an Indian falling off his pony. Some of our men determined to keep our traps and gear gave fire, but they were soon finished. The Indians saw the smoke from the gunshot and made quick work of the trapper foolish enough to shoot."

We stayed submerged for nearly an hour or so while those redskins cleaned out our camp. They rounded up our horses, gathered all our gear, and collected their dead. We got six of them and they kilt three of us before taking off with our stuff. We didn't come out of our cover 'til we heard the death howl. It ain't something I'm liable to forget. Whooping and moaning like banshees. With the bodies of their dead laid out on their ponies, they finally left us to what was left of our dinner."

"Lucky you made it out of that one," I said.

"Yea, that's why we come here hoping the Indians aren't such a problem."

"Not yet anyway," I explained. "Black Kettle is a peace chief. He's got the Cheyenne and Arapaho listening to him, but there are the Dog Soldiers who have been wreaking havoc."

"I heard about them. Paint themselves up like devils, scalpin' women and children," Jody piped in.

"Yea, but they are mostly in the plains attacking the wagon trains, not here. But we could run into a hunting party. Need to keep an eye out," I replied.

We hunted, trapped, and fished all the summer of '64. It was a good time for me. It was running into August when it was my turn to deliver meat to the fort in Denver. With six bucks loaded onto Hardtack I headed out. Things were still tense between my father and me, but I wanted to give my mother some of my earnings from the beaver pelts I gathered up over the summer.

When I arrived home, my father stepped out on the porch and stopped me from entering. He stood with his arms crossed over his chest and feet spread wide.

"Why are you here, Boy?"

"I came to give you some money from my summer's trapping," I said.

"Did you hear about what happened on the Overland Trail while you was holed up in the mountains?"

“No. What happened?” I asked, afraid it was another Indian raid.

“Indians attacked a wagon train and killed fifty-three settlers. Scalped and mutilated the bodies of women and children. They are moving in. I don’t want your mother, brothers, and sisters to be found the same way.” He glared at me as though it was my fault. I didn’t know what to say, so I just looked at the ground.

“Gov. Evans is calling for every able-bodied man to join up in the militia for 100 days. He’s called in the ‘friendlies’ for a talk. I think that means your friend Black Kettle.”

My mother overheard our talk and appeared in the doorway behind my father. As she wiped her hands on her apron, I saw the worry in her face.

“Alright, I will sign up if they will take me,” I said. I handed Father my poke and left.

The tension in the dusty streets of Denver was palpable. I plucked the notice off the bulletin board at the fort calling for men to sign up for 100 days. Most of the men who did were miners who had gone bust when the gold mines tapped out. They were a rag tag bunch, inexperienced fighters without proper equipment, and in line for a free meal. Winter was coming on, so Billy Jo and Jody signed up along with other mountain men.

Black Kettle and White Antelope, another peace chief, met with Colonel Whynkoop at Fort Lyon according to Gov. Evans' demand. The Indians agreed to surrender to the military and relocate if that would bring peace for their people. Major Wynkoop assured them it would. He told them to wait for him at Sand Creek until he could talk to the appropriate authorities. The Indian Agency was located at Fort Lyons. Many Indians were camped nearby to collect restitution from the government for loss of their land. Wynkoop allowed them to be fed leftover army rations. He was summarily discharged from his post on the grounds that he was too soft on the Indians. Evans appointed Colonel John Chivington, an honored war hero, in charge of all the troops including the "Hundred Dayers."

Chivington and Evans were both politically ambitious men who shared similar views about the Indian problem. Evans believed eradication was the answer. Chivington was in accord. He said, "Until the Indians were wiped out there could be no peace in the West."

He led his troops, including the Hundred Dayers, on a march from Denver to Fort Lyon where we garnered four howitzers. On November 28th, his band of six hundred men marched all night from Fort Lyon to Sand Creek. A regiment of one hundred men was led by Col. Silas Soule. Black Kettle was camped there with about five hundred of his people sleeping in 130 lodges. The men on foot were passing the bottle all night to fend off the cold. Many of them were drunk when we arrived at Sand Creek that morning. The stars and stripes and a white flag were flying on Black Kettle's teepee when Chivington pranced before the troops astride his stallion, brandishing his saber yelling, "Remember the Hungate family. Have no mercy on these red devils. Take no prisoners. Kill them all!"

And so, the Sand Creek Massacre had begun. Armed with rifles, the cavalry thundered down upon the village. They attacked the sleeping Cheyenne before dawn opening fire on fleeing women and children. They chased them down on their horses jumping down long enough to scalp them and take a coup as a bloody souvenir. Mob rule took hold of the Hundred Dayers and the men let loose the anger and resentment boiling inside them. Chivington had successfully unleashed their rage against innocents who had done them no harm.

The young warriors were away on a hunt. There was no one to defend The People. Some of the elder chiefs fled up Sandy Creek while a few women were able to hide in holes they dug in the creek wall. Colonel Soule was unwilling to fire upon innocents. Disgusted by what he was seeing, he held his regiment in check. I stood with them frozen, stunned by what was happening. Black Kettle was told they were safe here from the whites and that they were to wait here until the soldiers came relocate to them. Instead, the military men were cutting off ears, noses, private parts and hacking up the bodies of the dead.

I saw a woman running from a soldier on horseback. I saw she was with child. At that moment the solder shot her in the back, and she fell to the ground. The woman looked up in my direction and I saw that it was Shining Moon! The soldier got down from his horse rolled her over to face him, slit her belly open, then stabbed her baby with his saber and lifted it in the air. My whole body recoiled in horror. A guttural howl rose from my belly. I raised my rifle to my shoulder preparing to shoot the soldier that had killed Shining Moon when Captain Soule ordered his men to contain me. He was not for slaughtering innocents, but he wasn't for shooting our own solders either. They grabbed me by both arms. I fought to get free but was overpowered. When they finally did release me, I turned away from the horror before me, and then I ran. I ran and ran until I collapsed somewhere between Sandy Creek and Fort Lyon and vomited my guts out.

In the days that followed this heinous act,

Chivington wrote to his superiors that his “men waged a furious battle against well-armed and entrenched foes, ending in a great victory.” The returning troops holding scalps, and tobacco pouches made from the breasts of Cheyenne women held high in parades for locals to see perpetrated this lie. The people of Denver heralded them as heroes having saved them from the red skins.

Colonel Silas Soule sent a letter to superiors in Washington telling him that Chivington’s report was a lie.

“Hundreds of women and children were coming towards us and getting on their knees for mercy,” he wrote, “only to be shot and to have their brains beat out by my men professing to be civilized.”

Soule was prepared to testify in a hearing resulting from his letter, but he was shot in the head by one of the good folks in Denver who didn’t want to hear his story.

I am grateful not to have ever seen Running Deer again. I think he must have joined up with the Dog Soldiers. I could not bear to tell him what I saw, and that I had done nothing to stop it from happening. I live with the guilt that I did not go to Shining Moon’s aid, and, worse, that I did not retrieve her body or that of her unborn child. It is a sin that haunts my dreams and will forever make me ashamed.

Part Three

Isabella enters Estes Park

Colorado, 1873

Guardian of the Mountains

I rode in the direction Gabe told me was the way to Evans Lodge. Shortly, I came upon a crude cabin with smoke spiraling from a rock chimney. There was a pretty mare hobbled in the meadow and a white mule grazing free. The cabin looked more like an animal's den than a home. The mud roof was covered with furs of beaver and lynx and part of a deer carcass hung in a tree nearby. A sleeping black dog with the head of a mastiff rose and began barking at my approach. Skeletal remains of animals lay all about, but this disarray was nothing compared to the ruffian that emerged from his lair.

A broad-shouldered man about six feet tall wearing a tattered collection of furs and skins walked towards me. As he came closer, I saw he was wearing a scarf to hold up his pants made of skins. He wore another belt with a hunting knife and revolver strapped to his waist. On his feet a frayed pair of moccasins.

"Good afternoon madam," came from the

bedraggled recluse. I couldn't help staring at the flap of flesh drooping over his right eye socket. Not wanting to offend, I averted my gaze from his damaged countenance. As he got closer, I saw he had a three-day stubble on his chin, and I could smell spirits on his breath.

"What brings you to Muggins' Gulch?" he asked glaring at me with one bright blue eye.

I knew this must be the infamous Rocky Mountain Jim but did not let him know his notoriety preceded him. He may once have been a devilishly handsome man, but gross deformity spoiled his appearance. In addition to missing his right eye, there was a deep purple gash from his chin to his forehead disfiguring the entire right side of his face.

"I am looking for Evans Lodge."

"And who might you be?" he asked, sounding rather quarrelsome.

"I am Isabella Bird."

"Well, Miss. Bird, I am James Nugent at your service," he said removing his beaver skin cap and making a sweeping bow.

"You need to give me twenty-five cents to cross my land to get to Evans Lodge," he said.

Shocked at his lack of hospitality I replied, "Are you no more than a common highwayman?"

"A highwayman perhaps, but not common," he said with mischievous grin.

"You can't be serious about your fee."

"Indeed, I am madam. I am but a volunteer and need the revenue from passersby to save these mountains, but I will take to you the Evans place for free." He smiled broadly, possibly at his own generosity.

"Saving the mountains from what? Men like you?"

"Why, no madam, from your countrymen."

He obviously recognized that I was an English country woman. I decided to tell him my true mission.

"I am looking for a guide to take me up Longs Peak."

"It's too late in the season," he said eyeing me from top to bottom. "You look to be on the scrawny side. I doubt you have the goods to make the climb."

"How can you judge my mettle at one glance? I got here as soon as I could and I am willing to take the risk," I said, defending my desires.

"Nice that you are so willing to die, but I'm not in a big hurry to meet my maker."

With that he turned and whistled to his mule. "Biscuit, come!"

The mule ambled over to him. He left where we stood and grabbed a halter from a rail on his makeshift stable. With ease, he hopped on the saddleless mule, held up an arm and signaled me to follow. The dog followed wagging a happy tail. I ambled behind the swaying rump of his mule on a meandering trail to a knoll overlooking Evans Lodge resting in an idyllic valley below.

"This is as far as I go madam. I hope you enjoy your stay in Estes Park."

"What about your fee?"

"You will have to pass my land when you leave. I will collect the toll which will be doubled when you return," he said with a lopsided grin.

His flippant air amused me; being extorted did not.

"Very well. Thank you for escorting me Mr. Nugent."

"My pleasure Miss Bird." With that he turned his mule about and left me to contemplate my future home.

Estes Park is nestled in pine-sheathed mountains that skirt a lake flashing fandangos in the midday sun. My spirits soared as I approached Evans Lodge. The lodge and two smaller cabins of rough-hewn timber rested in the center of a broad meadow. A few horses grazed freely nearby. Griff Evans, a short, jolly-looking Welshman and two sheep dogs came out to greet me.

"Welcome ma'am! We don't get many ladies here! "Come on in and see if we are to your liking. Our man will take care of your horse."

I followed him into the lodge. A blazing fire in the hearth gave the great hall a welcoming glow. Several men lay about on the wooden plank floors smoking pipes and resting from a day outdoors. The smell of bread baking sharpened my appetite. Soon Mrs. Evans appeared wiping her hands on her apron.

"We got room if you're interested in staying. One of the boarders just packed up and left the cabin down by the lake open. It would cost eight dollars for the week and that includes meals and feed for your horse," she said.

I was thrilled at the thought of privacy along with good company at the end of the day during my stay. "That sounds perfect. I've been in the saddle all day. I'd like to see my cabin and freshen up."

"Sure thing. Come with me," she said.

What a joy to have my own cabin resting on the edge of a sparkling lake. The music of the river flowing down from the distant mountains quickened my pulse. Inside the cabin, Spartan furnishings included a tin basin, two towels, and a mirror. A mattress stuffed with hay covered by a handstitched quilt would be my bed. The chinks between the logs were not sealed as they should have been so there was a noticeable draft. The door was so swollen it wouldn't shut all the way, but for me, in much need of solitude, this cabin was heaven. The lilt of birdsong, the chuckling voice of river nearby, and the chirp of the lesser creatures hiding in the woods was all the company I wanted. From my cabin I could see the notch you must pass through to summit Longs Peak holding reign over it all.

"Let me know if you need anything. Supper is ready at six and breakfast starts at six in the morning. I will ring the bell," Mrs. Evans said, leaving me to settle into my new quarters.

I strolled down to the lake and studied the reflection of fast-moving white clouds in the translucent water. I saw my own image there and could hardly recognize the sun-tanned face staring back at me. I was wind-blown and weathered, but I had made it to the Inner World. The air was crisp with the scent of pine. The whisper of the boughs swaying in a sharp breeze was comforting. I had reached my destination and it was all mine. I felt I had escaped from the eyes of people and their many expectations. I was not the preacher's daughter devoted to charitable work elected to spread the word of God. I was not a spinster that should be seeking a husband. I was not an invalid too weak to lift her head from the pillow. No, I was none of those things. I felt a deep sense of belonging to this moment. That I was where I longed to be. Free in my wildness.

I was too tired to join the others for the evening and succumbed to an early slumber. After scribbling a letter to Hennie to let her know I had arrived safely, I drifted to sleep with dreams of exploring my new domain in the morning. But not all was well in paradise. I was awakened by a snuffling sound rising from below the floorboards. Then scratching as though someone buried alive was trying to claw free of their casket unnerved me. What could it be? A man? No room for that beneath the cabin. Besides, he would just come through the unlocked door. A bear? The fiercest beast in the wild would not bother to hide and wouldn't fit beneath the cabin. Then what? I was frozen in my fear of the unknown. I lay there wishing it away and praying for dawn to come. The mystery of the dark finally left with the golden light of a new day shining through my tiny window. I splashed icy water on my face, dressed hurriedly, and went to the lodge for breakfast grateful my hair had not turned white in the night.

A fire was blazing in the stone hearth, and the hall was bustling with guests enjoying a round of bacon, eggs, and potatoes. Mrs. Evans brought to the long table fresh coffee with real cream, and toast with sweet butter. A veritable feast.

"How'd you sleep Miss Bird?" Mr. Evans asked.

"Like the dead, until I was awakened by the scratching from the beast beneath my cabin. I almost came to get you."

"Ha! He laughed and slapped his thigh. "I forgot to tell ye…there's a skunk den beneath the cabin. Can't do nothin' about it. Disturbing those critters is worse than living with them. By the way, you can call me Griff," he added.

"Ya can't kill them or the stink will run you out. I saw a dog rub his nose to bleedin' trying to get rid of the scent," said a wiry Scotsman named Edwards at the end of the table.

Edwards and his wife shared the homestead with the Evans and helped with farming and running a herd of cattle. A young man wearing an English riding habit was introduced as "The Earl," and an American couple Mr. and Mrs. Dewy displayed culture and character I would welcome anywhere. Mr. Dewy was here for the camp cure and she was the dutiful wife at his side. Two other men were hunters, and one man was a miner from Silverton. A black man named Nate lives here all year taking care of the place in winter He was tall, muscular, and in his prime. Griff's daughter, a melancholy girl of about sixteen, helped Mrs. Evans serve the food. Edwards' children, a girl that looked to be about eight and a boy about ten, completed my company.

"So, I am living in *his* house?" I said.

"That's about right ma'am. You got to respect the wildlife around here. They were here first," Griff laughed heartily at his own joke.

"Does my host or hostess have a name?"

"Polecat suits him best, but you can give him a better one if you like," Griff said.

"I shall call him Sir Snuffles, as he does rule the manor."

"We will be needing supplies for a couple of days. Can you put together some grub for us?" asked one of the hunters, a tanned young man wearing a buckskin shirt and red bandana.

"Sure. Where you boys heading?" asked Mr. Edwards.

We were planning on going up to North Park. Heard there is plenty of elk there."

"Yes, there are plenty of elk and plenty of Indians who think they belong to them," Edwards said.

"The only white man welcome there is Mountain Jim," Griff added. "By all accounts he fathered two half breeds with a squaw named Falling Water."

"Now you don't know that for certain," Mrs. Evans said.

"Well don't matter," said Griff. "You know he's an Indian lover."

"Haven't heard of trouble lately, but don't start any is my advice," Griff added.

"Thought the Cheyenne had pretty much given up," the young man replied.

"Maybe go to Middle Park instead. No redskins there," suggested Edwards.

"Thanks for the warning. We will keep our eyes peeled," said the young man pushing away from the table. "Reckon will get an early start so we won't see you in the morning."

"I would like to hire a guide to take me to the summit of Longs Peak," I said, hoping for a better answer than the one Mr. Nugent gave me.

"The only one can do that is Mountain Jim," Nate replied.

"Yea, but he's a scoundrel and not to be trusted with a lady," Griff said.

"As long as he's not drinking, he is fine," Mrs. Evans chimed in.

"Stop defending him, woman," growled Mr. Evans, silencing his wife.

I let the topic rest. Eager to explore, I excused myself from good company.

My first day was spent surveying on foot. I staked Birdie in a meadow with knee-high grass letting her have a well-deserved rest. It felt good to walk and use different muscles, letting my calves and knees flex after the taxing thirty-mile ride from Longmont. I crunched across sparkling hoarfrost clinging to the grass in the meadow on the way down to the lake's edge. Dark green mountains cloaked in pine with gray monarchs streaked in white beyond rippled in the still waters. I splashed my face with the bracing water and filled my canteen.

This serendipitous walk took me along the lake's edge into sublime, un-surveyed wilderness. The nearest homestead is about eighteen miles distant. With the exception of Mountain Jim's cabin four miles away, there are no other human marks on nature. The Rocky Mountains are filled with many valleys, large and small, with heights varying from 6,000 to 11,000 feet. Remote North Park held by hostile Indians, Middle Park famous for hot springs, and South Park at 10,000 feet is a great rolling grassland seventy miles long. There are many more unnamed, known only to hunters and trappers. Estes Park at 7,500 feet is the fairest with glorious sunsets, sunny afternoons, and well-grassed meadows.

The soil is dry, gravely decomposed granite. Water doesn't settle here. It sifts through the soil. Even if it snows, the dusting is gone by noon. As I walked the rim of the lake, I met a gurgling rill snaking through the tall grass. It tumbled over rocks to join the glacier-fed Mirror Lake. It meant taking off my boots and dipping toes into the frigid flow. I found a comfy rock to rest on while waiting for my tingling feet to dry. Birdsong, the chuck of gray squirrels, and the chatter of the creek created a lovely melody. I arrived here too late for the wildflower season that only lasts a couple of months. Still, I spied a tender lavender blue columbine with a yellow burst in the center lifting to greet the morning sun.

I carried on my explorations and came upon a wetland where yellow blooms of skunk cabbage spread their glory on green pads as big as dinner plates. Standing in the middle of the scene was a magnificent moose with a giant crown of nature's making. He lifted his head pulling up reeds and dripping water from his grinding molars. His gaze rested on me. He seemed unalarmed by me being in his world, but I was shaken by his massive presence. I skirted around him amazed at the height and breadth of the creature. This truly is the realm of the beasts.

Looming in the distance, I could see the snow-slashed shoulder of Longs Peak. My intense desire to know God's pulpit encouraged me to speak with Mr. Nugent about the prospect of taking me to the summit during my stay here. The hike to his cabin was an easy one through the forest of dark green ponderosa pine. All the trees here except for the occasional grove of aspen are conifers dropping pine needles and making a thick, soft duff for footing. His cabin rests at 9,000 feet overlooking the valley where Evans Lodge sits 2,000 feet below, so it called for a climb. I was a little weak and light-headed due to the altitude, but it felt good to breathe deeply of the thin, dry curative air.

A grey stream of smoke spiraling from the rough rock chimney told me Mr. Nugent was home. As I drew near, his guard dog charged towards me at top speed. Being on foot made me much more vulnerable to his angry attack. Fortunately, his master appeared in time to divert disaster.

"Ring. Come!" he called.

The dog instantly pulled short and returned to the foot of his master who looked out of sorts. He was wearing his deer hide pants with unbuttoned long underwear for a shirt exposing blonde curls on his chest. He stood barefooted and waited for me to get close enough for conversation. As I neared, I saw that his good eye was ringed in red with dark circles making him look worn and haggard. He coughed and spat to the side at my approach.

"You shouldn't sneak up on a man, Miss Bird. You are liable to get shot."

"I wasn't sneaking. I am simply out for a walk."

"What made you walk in my direction, pray tell?"

The devoted dog at his side never took his eyes off his master while we spoke waiting for his next command.

"I am told you are the only one who can take me up Longs Peak."

"That's true."

"Well, I am happy to pay you a fair sum for your trouble."

"Money won't do you any good on the mountain, madam."

"Then what will prompt you? Even though I have arrived a bit late in the season, the weather seems fair," I said.

"The mountain makes its own weather, and it can change in moments," he replied.

"I see."

"You don't look like you weigh more than ninety pounds soaking wet, but I don't want to have to carry you out," he said, giving me another critical once-over.

"I assure you I can carry my own weight," I countered with a confidence I couldn't trust.

"Besides, what if I get hurt? Can you carry me out?" he asked, beginning to soften his gruff demeanor.

"No, I suppose not," I said. "Well, if you

change your mind I'm staying in the cabin by the lake."

"I know where you are," he said with a grin that made me uncomfortable.

Dinner that night was jolly. Griff, who has a taste for drink, was in a raucous mood. Edwards, as taciturn as Evans was gay, did not join in the merriment. I got the impression he was not happy with Griff's free-wheeling ways. Griff had claimed the homestead and built the lodge, but Edwards owned half of the thousand head of cattle, tilled the field where potatoes were planted and took care of the livestock. Griff tended to the guests, leading them on hunting and fishing trips and going into the Denver for supplies.

A tight-lipped cowboy from Montana named Buck arrived that day. Buck, the hunters, and "The Earl" lay on the floor before the roaring fire smoking their pipes. The children, calm after dinner, played games by the fire. I claimed a rocker by the warming blaze and mended my tattered Hawaiian riding dress. Edwards' wife and Mrs. Evans took off their aprons and joined the group after a long day of routine and unending chores. Griff pulled out his accordion and led us in a rousing chorus of songs. Conversation turned to the weather, which is the most important topic here.

"Looks like it will be clear tomorrow," came from Mr. Edwards who refrained from joining us in song.

"Yep. Think it will be good time round up the cattle and do some branding before they get snowed in," Griff said.

"Miss Bird, how would you like to join in a cattle roundup? We could use another hand."

"Yes, that would be wonderful!" I jumped at the chance to see more of the back country.

"If you boys want to make a few dollars, be ready to ride by seven in the morning seven."

Cattle Call

I awoke to the drumming of a woodpecker on the pine tree outside my window. The golden dawn eclipsed into a spray of pink and lemon yellow. Five deer with white bottoms up sipped water from the crystalline lake. There were three does and two yearlings as tame as if they were raised on a village green. Soon, a buck with a regal rack came to join his harem.

Eager with anticipation for the roundup, I had barely slept. Birdie was as excited as I was to get on with the day. Energized, refreshed, and eager, she pranced and chomped at the bit. I rode in a secure, deep-seated saddle wearing my Hawaiian riding dress and Turkish bloomers. The Earl turned up in English riding habit riding a high-born horse in light-weight English tack. I feared for him in such an insecure saddle. From my days in Hawai'i, I knew how treacherous wild cattle can be. Buck rode a quarter horse trained to corner cattle. He sported a lariat on the horn of a well-worn western saddle. Griff led the way on a raw-boned gelding with powerful haunches. His horse was not much to look at, but serviceable in the mountains. Nate was on an appaloosa mare, a spotted Indian pony, in a military stock saddle. We were all provided leather guards over our feet and lunch in a pouch slung over the saddle horn with the exception of Earl who wore a pack around his waist. Four large spotted hounds accompanied us.

With a “Tally Ho” from Griff our cavalry was off.

He charged ahead at a full gallop across the vast meadow of Estes Park letting the horses and riders feel their oats in the frosty morning air. I glanced over my shoulder to see Mountain Jim on a knoll overlooking the valley astride his white mule like a ghost rider watching us slip away. To reach the scene of the drive at a higher elevation, we slowed to make a climb up a rocky track and then a treacherous descent into another park watered by two rapid rivers. Peaks rising to 14,000 feet scarred by deep ravines open here to summer pasture lands. That is where the cattle become snowbound in winter if they are not herded out in time. There are about 2,000 cattle roaming the mountains that are as feral as any wildcat. A bull leads them Indian file to water and stands guard watching for predators as they drink. The bulls are cagy and take advantage of dodgy ground when being pursued. They are as volatile and dangerous as the shaggy buffalo that once roamed here. The cows must be tamed before they can be milked and even then, they give very little cream for the effort.

"Miss Bird, you, Nate, and Buck will go up canyon and drive the beef down to us. Earl and I will go up the one yonder. Push 'em down here and we will drive them together. Edwards will be waiting for us at the branding spot at the meadow gate with hot irons," Griff bellowed.

Thus began a grueling day of dodging death. I followed Buck who started out on the level at a gallop, leaping over trunks of downed trees on the way up canyon. After a few miles of avoiding rocks in the trail and splashing through creeks, we finally came across a herd tucked deep into the dead-end canyon. The bull picked up our scent and rallied his charges. Buck took the lead swinging his lariat overhead behind the cattle that were now bawling with alarm.

"Get up cows!" he barked.

"Nate, get to the right of them!" Buck commanded. Nate took his orders in stride and held his own in the race to get the cattle back to the open pastures.

"Miss Bird, you get to the left," Buck yelled to me over the din of the bleating cattle.

The cows cornered themselves in a rock-strewn, dry river corridor with steep and unstable footing that called for risky maneuvers. Birdie was magnificent with her iron legs and heart of gold. Fearless, she charged at the cows giving them no chance to bolt from the herd. The bull turned on Buck trying to gore his horse with massive, curled horns. Buck's cowpony side-stepped the animal and spared himself and Buck from a nasty injury. It took a couple of hours to herd about eighty head of cattle down the tight ravine to where Griff was waiting in the meadow.

Griff and the Earl had gathered another group of about forty cows. We knotted our bridles over the saddle horn and ate our lunch without dismounting. The rest of the afternoon was a blur of adrenaline-charged riding. We started over the level at a full gallop. In between heading off a deviant bovine, we dashed madly down hillsides, forded deep, rapid streams, saw lovely lakes and views of unsurpassed magnificence. We startled a herd of elk lazing in tall grasses as we rode at the very base of Longs Peak. The sun was hot, the air crisp. It was the most exhilarating ride of my life. More daring than daunting. More exciting even than my rides in the Islands.

Emerging from this euphoria we came upon the sight of a thousand long-horned Texan cattle feeding in a valley below us. Our cows aimed to join them. They started to move in unison towards the other herd.

Griff yelled to us to head ’em off.

“Nate and I will take the cows we got collected to the branding site. You, Buck, and Earl get down there and cut out as many as you can and bring ’em to us,” he ordered.

And away we went at a hard gallop downhill! I could not hold Birdie back; she was overcome with the herd instinct of her race. Down-hill, up-hill, leaping over rocks and timber. The horses dashed at racing speed trying to overtake one another. Dizzied and breathless by the pace I feared Birdie would break a leg, but she kept up with Buck without incident. The dogs were with us now helping to round up the herd. A bull turned on one of them hooked the animal with his great horns and threw it into the air. The dog was stunned but managed to pick itself up and continued herding the cows like a sheep dog. With a whoop and a holler we cut a part of the larger herd and drove them to the branding site. At the end of the day, we had collected about 200 head for Evans. The stink of burning fur is not one I care to remember, but it is the way of the

West to singe the hide of cattle to claim them as your own.

After the long, arduous day, I had supper and went early to bed. The next morning, I was startled by a light knock on my door.

Mountain Jim stood there wearing his black eye patch.

"Good morning, Miss Bird." He turned his face slightly to the side as he addressed me so I might be spared the sight of his disfigurement.

"Good Morning, Mr. Nugent, what news have you for me?"

"Mr. and Mrs. Dewy have requested I guide them on a ride to the Hot Springs. I thought after your day of cattle rustling you might enjoy a soak. Would you like to join us?"

Much amazed at this invitation, it took me a moment to respond.

"Of course, that would be lovely."

"Good. We leave around nine," he said, smiling brightly. "Bring your bathing costume. I will tell Mrs. Evans to pack you a lunch," he said, leaving me wondering about this generous turn of events.

The leisurely start gave me time to groom Birdie. She had behaved admirably and deserved a good rub. I circled the curry on her muscled rump lifting dust from her fine black coat. She loved having her back where the saddle rests brushed vigorously. She seemed to sigh with lazy gratitude as I gave her long strokes across her withers and down her legs. What a beauty she is and such a good friend. So responsive and brave. She nickered when I rubbed the base of her throat, a spot impossible for her to reach on her own. I rode her in a light snaffle. She did not need diabolic bits or spur to do her job. She had been trained by voice, love, and attention as seems to be the Western way.

After the stimulating ride yesterday, I was happy to fall in line behind Mr. and Mrs. Dewy on a trail ride. She was riding cavalier style to keep up with her consumptive husband who loved to be outdoors. Mr. Nugent led the way on Biscuit without benefit of saddle. He had a simple saddle bag thrown over her withers carrying supplies for the day.

We ambled across the high grass meadow edging the lake to a hint of trail that ducked into the forest lined with pitch pine and a ground-hugging shrub. Flashes of blue swept by as jays darted through the understory to light on a limb where they watched us pass through their territory. I saw Biscuit's muscled haunches tuck into a forested trail that began our climb. It was a crisp September day with the scent of fall in the air. We passed through a grove of aspens. Their round leaves shimmied to gold in the white shafts of light filtering through the trees.

I heard the voice of an energetic creek ahead. Jim held up one hand signaling us to wait until he had made the crossing. The unflappable mule entered the plunge without hesitation. Jim gave her full rein so she could find her way. She tested the boulder footing with a hoof before going forward. She waded slowly through the roiling brew, then jumped out on the other side.

"Just get them in the creek and let them feel their way," Jim instructed.

It was our turn to follow. Mrs. Dewy was hesitant, but her horse was a steady ride and took care of her. Birdie was wonderful. She snuffled the water and marched bravely through to the other side. Across the creek, the path became less defined. Pocked with sharp rocks, it twisted through the pines. At times we were traversing huge slabs of granite and climbing on a stairway of stone. We came upon a rockslide that covered the trail, so we had to bushwhack our way around it. I worried for Birdie on this rocky footing. The trail became a bare scratch on the earth forcing us to stay close behind Jim. We passed a gushing waterfall foaming white over glistening rocks and sending up a cooling spray.

After an hour or so, we entered a gorge on a narrow ledge backed by a staggering wall of rock striated with orange and vermilion. Below, a raging river clogged with downed trees carved the corridor still deeper. One slip here would be disastrous, but with Biscuit at the helm the horses remained calm. Once through that terror, we came upon a cascade of white falling from 500 feet into staggered rock pools that spilled water onto the trail and over the ledge into the river below.

"You can give 'em a drink here," Jim said.

Water pulsed up Birdie's neck as she sucked in the pure glacier-fed pool. I was beginning to feel light-headed due to a touch of altitude sickness. I drank greedily from my canteen then filled it at the pool.

We emerged from the gloom of the gorge to an expansive view of craggy gray summits splotched with white patches of snow. I felt I was in a landscape painting inspired by Albert Bierstadt and others who had tried to capture the ephemeral beauty and serenity of these peaks.

Jim held up his hand once more signaling us to halt. He turned to face us and pointed to our destination.

"Down there is where we stop for lunch. The hot springs are behind that cluster of boulders. You ladies can put on your swim costumes there and enjoy a soak. Mr. Dewy and I will take a turn after."

We each found a boulder to sit on, opened our lunch sacks, and enjoyed a simple lunch of jerky and bread. There was no graze here for Birdie, so I tied her to a tree where she could rest in the shade.

Eager to slip into the curative waters, I stripped off my Hawaiian riding dress and put on a blouse that insured modesty. Steam rose from the turquoise pool framed in round boulders. I gave the thermal spring the toe test and found it wonderfully tolerable. I entered slowly feeling the bottom comprised of granite pebbles with my feet. Satisfied it was safe, I sank into the steaming bath. My mind drifted back to my time in the hot pools of Hawai'i. I remembered the loving hands of Melanie who gave me lomi-lomi massage to release the reservoir of pain in my heart and body. Now, my aches and bruises from a month of rough riding were eased by the warmth of nature's remedy. I recalled the bruising fall at Chalmers', the exhausting ride to Estes Park along the St. Vrain River, and the adrenaline-spiked roundup of yesterday. Silently, I gave thanks that my back did not call me back to being a bed-ridden invalid. Those days were behind me! I was becoming stronger with each breath of the intoxicating mountain air.

The ride home was at an easy pace that let me soak in the landscape. When we reached Evans Lodge, I thanked the Deweys for letting me join them.

"Thank you, Mr. Nugent, no day was more welcome," I said.

"My pleasure madam. It is good to be with someone who loves the mountains for the mountains. Not just for the bounty of furs or food." With that he tipped his beaver hat and turned Biscuit towards his solitary home.

At breakfast, Griff announced that he was going to Denver for supplies.

"I'll be taking Mrs. Evans and my daughter with me. We spend the winter at our farm on the plains."

"I see. Would it be possible for you to pick up a few things for me while you are there?"

"Sure, just don't' ask me to be buying you any personal lady's items."

"Is a pair of boots too personal? Mine are worn thin."

"No ma'am. I should be able to do that. Draw me a pattern of your foot and I will do my best."

I gave Evans a list of items and $100 to cover the cost of my purchases. He was also to be bring back mail and news from the outside world. I am mildly interested in the state of things but yearn more for a letter from Hennie whom I've not seen for almost a year. I gave him the packet of letters I had written to her journaling my time here. The mule-drawn wagon was loaded with furs to be traded. The route over the mountains was a precarious one that was filled with dangerous river crossings. With the crack of a whip, the mules surged forward and our lifeline to the outside set sail.

Knock at the Door

Nights around the fire now were less boisterous, but I enjoyed them even more. I mended my clothes that were falling to pieces and offered to mend a few things for the others. My father taught us to be charitable in all ways and darning socks was something I could do for the Edwards family and Nate, my constant companions. The Edwards' children, Sadie and Sam, lay beside the hearth playing games while the adults told stories.

Nate spoke of his days riding shotgun on a carriage bringing mail to Denver.

"We was rockin' and rollin' at a brisk pace, wheels spinning, driver crackin' the whip on six fine black horses when we was attacked by Injuns. They bore down on us whoopin' and hollerin'. They was painted up, so I knew they were serious. They was ridin' right next to us on their ponies streaked in bright red paint getting ready to let loose their arrows at us."

The children's eyes grew wide as he went on.

"The stagecoach was bouncing till I thought it would turn over. The passengers inside were being thrown from side to side.

"I took my shotgun and splattered them with buckshot. They was still comin' at us, so I took out my pistol and took straight aim at the leader holding a staff with scalps hangin' from it. He fell from his horse, and the others fell back and stopped to pick 'im up."

"And then what?" the children urged.

"Well, then we just kept rolling and here I am today to tell you I'm done with being a soldier." Nate laughed and slapped his knee.

"Were you a soldier?" I asked. Nate was a Negro, so I wondered how that could be.

"Yes, ma'am. I was a Buffalo Soldier in the Union Army. When the war ended in '66 there wasn't any work for a black man in the South, so I came west. We were a segregated unit that wasn't afraid of a fight. We were made guardians of the stagecoaches, protected settlers coming west in wagon trains, and escorts to the Indians being relocated. General Custer refused to have blacks in his regimen. So that's why I lived to tell about it. Otherwise, I'd be pushin' up daisies like the rest of his men." He laughed at that revelation.

"What of Jim?" I asked Nate. "How did he get here?"

“Nobody really knows too much about Jim, but I do know he seen too much killin’. He was at the massacre at Sand Creek in ’64.”

“I’ve not heard of that.”

“Most people won’t talk about it. They are ashamed of things that happened there. Keep it covered up.”

“What things?”

“Things too vile for a lady’s ears,” he said, ending our talk.

The routine of my day had grown calm. Breakfast at six, back to my cabin where I wrote letters to Hennie describing the wonders around me or sketched the peaks trying to capture their celestial beauty. I could not duplicate the tenderness of the pink afterglow on the crags at the end of the day. There was still peacefulness to my days with the Evans and the hunters gone. A couple of campers stopped in, but they didn’t stay long. The days passed slowly. I wanted Evans to return with letters from Henrietta and news about the banks, but, in a way, I didn’t really care about what was happening outside of the park.

One chill morning, I awoke with snowflakes on my eyelashes and a dusting of snow on my coverlet. The snow had seeped through the unsealed chinks of the logs and settled in a fine mist on the floor. I blinked the frost away and swept the snow from the floor. The season was fast ending and still no word from Mr. Evans.

Then one evening while we sat around the fire there was a gentle rap at the door. Sadie ran to the door thinking it was Griff returned with gifts for her and Sam. But it was Jim Nugent and his dog Ring.

"Ma, Pa, it's Mountain Jim," Sadie said with great excitement grabbing his hand and pulling him towards the glowing fire.

"Good evening. I hope I'm welcome," he said.

Mr. Edwards rose to shake his hand, "Of course you are Jim, come in. Rest a spell."

Nate got up and gave him a bear hug. "Welcome brother."

Jim took off his fur jacket and beaver hat but kept is hunting knife in his vest pocket. He was wearing his eye patch. The children clamored around him, jumping on his broad shoulders playing with his curls. He gave them his attention first: grabbing Sam and swinging him about, and then tickling Sadie's belly making her giggle wildly.

Jim brought Ring with him, so pandemonium ensued until the sheep dogs calmed down. Ring curled up at the foot of his master with a contented sigh.

"What brings you to us?" asked Mr. Edwards.

Children, get off Jim," Mrs. Edwards said.

"I have some news for Miss Bird."

"Pray tell, what could that be?" With the first snow, I had given up all hope of summiting Longs Peak.

"Two fellas from Longmont came into my camp. They say they want to go up the mountain. I told 'em it was risky, but if they really wanted to go, I would take 'em, but only if you went with us," he said, looking directly at me for my reaction.

I wanted to give him a bear hug but held myself in check. "But, what of the snow? Mountain makes its own weather. What about all of that?" I asked.

"Well, it can be precarious this time of year, and you will have to dress for it, but I don't think it is too late. The weather is looking more settled and even if we don't get farther than the timberline, it will be worth going."

"Yes! Yes! And Yes," I cried. Bear hugs I could hold in check, but not my excitement. "When do we leave?"

"In the morning, madam. We will ride into Lily Lake and from there up to our camp at the base where we overnight."

"Mrs. Edwards, can you provide Miss Bird with some long trousers and a warm jacket and gloves?"

"Certainly, Jim," she replied.

"Will need some grub. Steaks, bread, sugar, tea, and butter enough for three days."

"I will take care of it," Mrs. Edwards said.

"Nate, you will have to come and get us if we aren't back in three days."

"Right. I don't want to be collectin' frostbit climbers. Be careful out there."

"Meanwhile, maybe we can have a little song out of you Nate," Jim said. Nate flashed a bright smile with white teeth against mahogany skin. He picked up his guitar and strummed it softly until he was ready to sing a song from his slavery childhood. His was a deep-throated melodious voice rich in tone. We were enthralled with the sad sweetness of his song.

When he was done, he handed Jim the guitar who took it and gently stroked a chord between each sentence as he shared his latest ode to the mountains.

"Take me to the mountain shrine / Where God's glory spreads unbound / Go to the mountains' splendor and walk among the beasts / Find your place among them in harmony and peace / Take me to the mountains where cold winds blow. / Show me the way to shelter in the pines on icy fields / Lay me there to rest in my twilight days of afterglow."

"Mighty pretty Jim, mighty pretty," said Mrs. Edwards, rocking peacefully in her chair beside the fire casting shadows on her weathered face.

"Thanks, ma'am," he said then turned to Nate. "Those boys wanted to know if you would dress their kill and smoke some of the meat while we are away."

"Sure, it will be ready for them when you get back," Nate said.

"Alright then, it's settled. They will bring it to you in the morning. Goodnight Miss Bird. Be ready to ride by seven," Jim said, and left.

Prayers Answered

I didn't sleep that night even though I knew I would need all my strength for the climb. I fretted over my weak ankles and prayed my back would not betray me. I asked for this journey and now that it was upon me, I was frightened that I would fail miserably and be caught out a fraud.

The two fellas turned out to be Gabe and Jake. They eyed me with disdain. It was obvious they were annoyed at having to take me with them up the mountain. Still, they were civil.

"Good mornin' Miss Bird. Looks like our paths are crossing again," Gabe said.

"Yes, and it looks to be a glorious day," I said, without malice, hoping they would warm to my company.

Mr. Nugent turned up looking the perfect ruffian. He had on an old pair of high boots with a shabby pair of baggy trousers made of deer hide cinched with a scarf, a leather shirt with three ragged waistcoats over it, and revolver in the top waistcoat pocket. His tawny ringlets were crushed beneath his beaver cap. His saddle was covered in skins with dangling paws. He had camp blankets behind, an axe and canteen hanging from the horn, and across all that, his rifle. His high-spirited Arab mare looked overmatched with all his gear aboard.

I had a stack of camp blankets behind me. My boots were worn and painful to walk in, so Mrs. Edwards lent me a pair of old hunting boots that hung from the horn on my saddle.

Even with the horses heavily loaded, Jim struck out at a gallop for the first half mile. Then he threw his horse on her haunches and dropped back beside me.

"You are getting your wish, my lady," he said and smiled.

I could not help but be charmed by his contradictions. Once a gruff ruffian and then a gentleman. Miss K had told me that if you treat Jim like a gentleman, you will find one. This seemed to hold true.

The ride was a series of glories and surprises. It was a crisp fall day with a hint of winter to come in the air. A stiff wind whipped the boughs of the ponderosas swaying and creaking overhead. It was a long, quiet trail winding through the protection of the trees. It gave me time to ponder the peace settling over the undisturbed stillness that was only broken by the ramblings of Mountain Jim who seemed to need to share his thoughts with me.

"Most people think the mountains are static, but they are ever changing. Shifting with the grumblings beneath the crust that lifts them to even greater heights. They are planed by the wind and carved by the rains and glaciers. They are living things," Jim said.

He spoke of the hidden goodness in the mountains. "You see, Miss Bird, no one owns the mountains. The Cheyenne, Arapaho, and Ute came here for a thousand years to hunt, but they never spoke of owning the land. No, they talked about the land owning them. They saw the creatures as brothers and learned from their ways. They walked softly on the land.

"Dunraven's scheme is to own the territory and turn it into a playground for the wealthy."

"Who is that and why is that so horrible?" I dared.

"If you enjoy spending time with a villain that would be a good idea. The Earl of Dunraven landed here from Ireland in '72. His family owns a great estate in Limerick. He inherited vast wealth he aims to use buying up land on the Front Range. He plans to turn it into a private game preserve for gentry to plunder for pleasure in the style of your estates in England. He has already bought up the holdings of the legal homesteads and now he has launched a scheme to get the land that's left."

"What kind of scheme?"

"He pays down-and-outs to homestead land not claimed. They build a lean-to or a rude log cabin and live there for a while to comply with the homestead laws. Then Dunraven buys the deed for $100, and they move on. Governor Hunt is helping him get away with this. He's been working on Evans to sell. But, I'm standing in the way."

Jim chuckled at this revelation.

"Only problem for Dunraven is he has to cross over my land to get to Estes Park. I'm about the only thing stopping him from owning everything you see here."

"No one can own the wildness of this place," I assured him.

The gentle ascent on the path through the pines became lined with aspen leaves scattered on the ground that looked like gold coins. These were the real riches of the mountains, not what the gold miners came from distant lands to extract. We entered the aspen grove with white trunks chinked in black as though a lumberman's axe had scarred them. Below they were wounded, but above their shivering leaves glowed in the shaft of light filtering through them. I saw myself there. The beginnings of my life wounded, but now wearing a crown of glorious yellow light. Rumi, a man of great wisdom, had said: "The wound is the place where the Light enters you." Was he speaking of the Light of God, or was it the light of self-knowledge?

After three hours of an easy march, we arrived at the Lake of the Lilies so named for the bright yellow blooms resting on green pads. Still waters reflected dark pines and the shimmering orange crags we would soon be scaling.

"We'll give the horses a rest here," Jim said, dismounting.

After a quick lunch, he asked me to take a stroll with him around the lake to a marsh where blackbirds swayed on the brown tufts of cattails The chorus of dragon flies, butterflies, and other buzzing creatures flitting about filled the air.

"I set traps for beaver here in the spring," Jim said. "It looks like still waters, but there is an underwater current that keeps the water fresh. Sometimes, if I'm lucky, I will see river otter playing here. I never take so many beaver that there won't be more for me to catch the next year."

From Lily Lake we ascended into the indigo gloom of pine forests that clothe the mountains up to about 11,000 feet. Ducking limbs that threatened to knock me off the saddle became a full-time occupation. On the narrow and rocky trail, tree trunks came dangerously close to banging my knees. I kept my legs pinned to Birdie's side as she plunged forward unconcerned about my dilemma. It was all I could do to stay astride as she lurched upward. The steep trail turned into scattered stones and jagged slabs of granite. Through the pines I glimpsed purple gorges and looming grandeur, but avoiding decapitation held my attention. There was an eeriness here. A stillness that had not seen the lumberman's axe. It was a land unto itself, with no mark of mankind. As we went higher, the trees grew smaller. Dead pines knocked down by fierce winds lay strewn about in jumbled heaps.

We finally reached our campsite where Longs Peak towered 3,000 feet above us. We picketed the horses and gathered pine boughs for our beds and dead wood for a fire. Gabe and Jake chose camp spots away from the fire. I found a shelter made of pines branches built by previous climbers. My saddle made a comfortable pillow. Jim built a raging fire to stave off the chill as twilight descended. Soon the afterglow came on turning the peaks a rosy hue. Gabe and Jake warmed to the occasion that night breaking out in song and telling stories about their hunt. Jim recited a poem of his own creation. “Amazing Grace” came to my mind and the men joined me in singing the hymn.

When it was time to turn in, Jim ordered Ring to go to my side. The dog instantly came to me and lay his massive head on my lap never taking his eye off his master. He served to be a warming blanket for me the rest of that cold night. At some point in the night, I was awakened by the caterwauling of a mountain lion that made Ring restless, but he did not leave me. A swirl of anxiety in the pit of my stomach would not let me go back to sleep. It was exciting to lie there beneath glittering heavens waiting for the sun to come up so we could start our climb.

At daybreak while I was tending to Birdie, Gabe came running. “Jim says, you got to come and see.”

I followed him to a ledge where Jim was standing. Below us, a massive blanket of gray clouds settled between the mountains. A sunburst of fire lit the sky. Before us, spread a dazzling display of gold, mauve, lavender, and deep purple streaked across the horizon.

Jim stood in silence. Finally, he looked at me and said, “There is a God.”

I was no less impressed with the visage, but more astounded that such a reckless character called us to embrace sublimity.

The Climb

We set off early hoping to be able to make the climb on foot and return by nightfall. It became apparent that the boots Mrs. Edwards gave me were more of a hindrance than a help navigating the rocky terrain. We came upon a camp where supplies were left behind by a man who had attempted the climb, but it appeared he was forced to abandon his effort. Luckily for me, there was a pair of boots among the equipment he left that I could wear. Soon, we were above the tree line that afforded majestic views, but the thin air was affecting our breathing. The only life here in the barren landscape are the yellow-bellied marmots that stood on hind legs barking at us as we passed.

We hopped from rock to rock until reaching the "notch," the gateway to the summit where it became a knife-blade-like ridge only a few feet wide covered with colossal boulders. From there, looking up, we could see the cavernous side of the peak composed of boulders and broken granite.

Awful chasms deep with ice and snow awaited the careless climber. Below, glacier-fed lakes sparkled like diamonds in the weak morning sun. North Park was off in the blue distance, along with Middle Park which was already closed for the season, and peaks spread to eternity.

Longs Peak towered two thousand feet above us. Thus began the real business of climbing. Smooth granite slabs with barely a foothold were made slick with pockets of snow. Many of the rocks were loose and tumbled at the touch. Jim roped me to him, but it was no use; I couldn't get traction and started slipping back down the trail. I felt miserable. It was obvious that Gabe and Jake were right; I was a danger to the party. I was prepared to turn back, but Jim hauled me up like a sack of potatoes until I could find footing.

"She's not going to make it," Jake said.

"She's going to get us killed," Gabe said.

"You boys can go back if you like, but Miss Bird and I are going to the top," Jim told them.

The men glared at me as though I was a murderess.

"I may be over my head," I said to Jim.

"You are coming with me. Now, you boys just try to keep up."

Gabe and Jake fell into step grumbling.

The way through the notch was blocked by

snow. We had to backtrack. Slipping, sliding, and straining every muscle in my body for two hours got us to two gigantic boulders called the Dog's Lift. We barely squeezed through. I had to climb onto Gabe's shoulders while Jim hauled me up from above. Slipping, faltering, gasping with throbbing hearts and panting lungs we finally reached 400 feet of vertical wall considered the most dangerous part of the ascent. Terror took hold has I looked down. One slip would land me in a bloody, lifeless heap. Ring, who had more sense than I, refused to come farther.

I scrambled to find footholds in cracks in the slick granite wall. I slipped and swung out into the void dangling from the rope that Jim held tight. Death's cold breath was upon me. He wound the rope around his waist, secured his footing and pulled me up to the top of the boulder wall saving me from a gruesome demise. Once I was aloft, he lifted me upon his broad shoulders and carried me along a ledge of rock that made me sick and dizzy. Finally, we reached the summit of Longs Peak where we were greeted by a buffeting wind.

Unmatched grandeur, majesty, and beauty stretching to infinity at last! Here, on what is a vast plateau, you are holding hands with God and taking in His vast creation. Snowy ranges, one behind the other, extend as far as the eye can see. Sleeping in a wintry embrace with snow patches, slashes, and scars are Pikes Peak, Grays Peak, and a host more of unnamed pinnacles. The exaltation combined with the humility I felt is beyond my powers of description. One might ask why I had to know God's pulpit. I can't answer it myself only to say the sense of wonder, complete wholeness, and satisfaction were mine for a few fleeting moments.

"The mountains dwarf humans. Puts them in their place," Jim said softly, as though talking to himself.

We couldn't stay long as Jake's lungs were bleeding and Gabe was suffering from mountain sickness. We were all thirsty from the dry air and we had run out of water.

"Can't eat snow. It will just make you thirstier," Jim said, back to his normal gruffness. "We've got to get going."

I was quite breathless. My arms felt as though they had been pulled out of their sockets, my legs were rubbery, but now we had to conquer the descent. The way down was even more treacherous than the way up. The vertical wall was as slick as polished marble. I had to get down on my haunches to avoid sliding to the bottom of the ravine where it connected to a rock ledge hugging the canyon wall. Jim went ahead of me so I could step down on his shoulders. Mountain sickness can be deadly. Gabe was breathless and struggling to keep up. Jake was coughing red splotches of blood on the snow.

"You boys can go down the way we came up. Miss Bird and I will take a longer, but easier way down. You need to get into lower elevations as quick as you can," Jim said, pointing out the way for them to go.

With that, they were off and out of sight in moments. The easier path consisted of hours on a trail of sharp rocks broken up with boulder hopping. By the time we reached camp, I was so exhausted I passed out on my pine-bough bed. I awoke in the middle of the night to see Jim staring into the fire with Ring's head resting in his lap. His demeanor was downcast. He looked the seat of despair. I moved to him to see if I could comfort him.

"Thank you, Mr. Nugent, for taking me up the mountain. You were right."

"How's that?" he said not lifting his gaze from the fire.

"You did have to carry me."

"It was you that carried me to the top for one more look at eternity," he said with the hint of a smile.

He was not wearing his eye patch. Flames cast ominous shadows across his disfigured face. Drawn to his deep melancholy, I came closer and gently placed my fingers on his scarred cheek. I sat down beside him by the hypnotic fire and took his hand in mine. The intensity of his deep sadness melted my resistance to his charms. This may have been a performance, but I believe he was genuinely downhearted.

"May I know what is troubling you so?"

"Nothing you can do anything about, I reckon," he said still staring into the flickering flames spitting sparks in the black night.

"Why are you so alone in this world? I was told you have children."

With that he jerked his head up and caught my questioning gaze.

I don't have any children I know about. If I did, I would want to be a part of their up-bringin'."

"How about you? Do you have children?"

Caught off guard by this question, I took my turn staring into the glowing embers for answers.

"No, I am not brave enough for that endeavor."

"You seem plenty brave enough to me," he laughed.

Then, he reached out to me, gently lifted my face to his and kissed me as softly as a whisper.

"My wounds are as deep as yours. They are just not as visible," I said.

"Is that what brought you to me?" he asked.

"I don't know, but I know you have helped me leave my past behind."

"You have made me remember what I'm fighting for," he said.

"And what is that?"

"Why, the mountains, of course. I'm the only one blocking the way of what some folks call progress."

He smiled tenderly at me and said, "Once you've been in the mountains, they become a part of you. Like the kiss of a lover."

With that, he drew me closer and kissed me deeply. I felt heat rising in my chest and a deep stirring in my belly unknown to me. I pulled away in confusion. Jim was a dangerous man with wild mood swings and degenerate habits. More than that, I have never known a man. I'm sure he could feel that about me. I flushed crimson with embarrassment.

"I'm sorry, I didn't mean to be so bold," he said pulling back. "Will you let me take you to some of my special places? I want you to love my mountains the way I do."

"Yes, that would be wonderful," I said, relieved he had changed the mood. I was frightened by what

I was feeling for him. This was impossible. It could not be happening.

On the ride back to Estes Park, ominous dark clouds swarmed overhead. Wicked gashes of lightning ignited the sky, and a terrible rumbling capped with an explosive clap of thunder told us we had gotten out of the high country just in time.

Next morning, I awoke to snowflakes on my eyelashes and snow dusting on my quilt. I smiled secretly at the knowledge I had made it to the top of the mountain before Mother Nature shut the doorway to heaven for the season. I learned later it was eight months before anyone dared to attempt to climb Longs Peak again.

Sacred Solitude

It's been ten days since Evans left for Denver. We are all anxious now for his return with supplies, mail, and news from the outside. The days tripped quietly one into another. I was content in my cabin overlooking the lake where I settled into a pleasant routine. From my bed in the early dawn, I looked out upon Mirror Lake in still, leaden repose. Then when bright orange flared through the peaks, the lake took on a shimmering golden glow. Blue jays stepped daintily on the sparkling hoar frost and gray squirrels lectured from the safety of the pines. Elk and deer come down to water as each day begins anew.

The mountains offer unsullied perfection. I didn't need more than what was in my cabin. In between trying to capture the wild beauty embracing me in sketches and in my letters to Hennie, I took hikes and rides into the forest. Then there was the glory of sunset and the showy afterglow on the face of the crags at day's end. I helped Mrs. Edwards with the many chores attendant to running the lodge: sweeping the floors, washing dishes, bringing in wood. Washing and mending my scant wardrobe always needed to be done. It was an easy life and one that soothed me, but the threat of snowstorms that close Estes Park from the rest of the world for the winter was upon me.

Each day I rode on the trail to Longmont hoping to see if Evans was returning with the money that would allow me to move forward with my plans to tour Colorado.

Instead of Evans, I ran into Mr. Nugent at his cabin.

"How would you like hike with me up to Loch Lake?" he asked.

"Yes, that would be grand," I said, again welcoming the opportunity to explore.

"I'll pack some grub for lunch." With that, he ducked back into his lair. He came out smiling brightly and tacked up his beautiful mare.

Without warning, he took off at a full gallop. Birdie raced to catch up and soon we were pounding neck and neck across the expansive meadow carpeted in knee-high grass. I stood in my stirrups like a jockey on a steeple chase and gave Birdie full rein. Tears streaming, blood pumping, heart thumping, we made a pretty picture with his curls flying and me in my tattered Hawaiian dress. He pulled up short and entered the dark green of the forest. I caught my breath on the easy amble through the pines. We walked quietly as Indians on the hunt, neither of us wanting to disturb the silence with chatter. There is a sameness in this vast landscape that soothes. It lacked the variety of foliage in Hawai'i but offered its own brand of loveliness in quietude.

"We will picket the horses here," Jim said, dismounting.

The first leg of the inviting path took us over a rough footbridge crossing a gurgling creek lined with lush grasses and maidenhair ferns. A stair-stepper climb led us to a charging cascade. Energetic water sliding over immense boulders carved a gorge framed in orange rock formations striated with mineral deposits. A rock formation that looked like a giant toadstool stood thirty feet tall from the river corridor floor with a flat, round pad about six feet wide on top. It was about three feet from the bank overlooking the raging torrent below. Jim hopped onto the flat pad and extended a hand.

"Care to join me," he asked with an impish grin.

One slip and I would be swirling downstream and smashed on the boulders below. In a giddy moment of insanity, I leaped to where he stood. He caught me and laughed loudly at my trembling.

“Thought you would like to feel the surge of the river instead of just looking at it,” he said.

He put his arm around my shoulder as we stood in the cooling mist generated by the water pounding into a pool below. I felt safe within his embrace. Soon, he jumped back to safety and I followed without hesitation this time.

The intoxicating air and the mystique of the crystalline alpine lake to come pulled me up the canyon. The mountainside trail consisted of rock steppingstones that led to more stunning vistas of granite precipices overlooking the river. The intense sun, thin air, and the altitude made me feel weak.

“I need to catch my breath,” I said sitting down beneath a shady pine.

“Take your time. We are in no hurry. In the summer, this trail is flush with wildflowers: lavender lupine, fire engine red penstemon, and yellow wallflower to name a few. Wish you could be here then,” he said somewhat wistfully.

We continued up the trail that turned into a narrow rocky ledge overlooking what had become a deep chasm carved by the river filled with boulder jumbles and downed trees. When we hit snow, I feared I had made a terrible mistake. Mr. Nugent took my arm and helped me through the slip-and-slide that was the last stretch of the trail opening to the vista of Loch Lake framed in gray granite walls.

The majesty of Loch Lake did not disappoint. I could see pink mountain trout swimming in the jade green, placid, chill waters. I took off my boots and dangled my toes in the invigorating glacier-fed lake feeling proud of myself for meeting the challenges of the hike. Resting on a boulder beside the lake breathing the crystalline air left me amazingly refreshed.

Jim put down a cloth on a boulder overlooking the lake beneath the shade of a pine and spread a simple lunch of venison jerky and bread. We drank deeply of the pure water and filled our canteens for the hike down. He was a perfect gentleman, of good cheer the entire day and never hinting at the gloom he had displayed at our camp at the base of Longs Peak. It was as though two people lived inside his skin.

"Now that you have conquered the Rockies, where will you go?"

"I am planning to tour the highpoints in Colorado around Denver and then on to New York. After that, I am thinking about China, Tibet. I'm not sure where I will venture from there."

"That's some big thinking. When do you plan to leave?"

"I am waiting for Evans to return with my funds."

"I wouldn't be trusting that polecat with my money if I were you," he said.

"I'm not in a position to argue. He should be back any day now."

"What do you expect to find in foreign outposts?"

"I don't know. I just know that I spent the first half of my life confined. Now, that I freed myself from the expectations of others and have strengthened my body, I shall live the last half as an adventuress."

"I've never met a woman like you," he said.

"Nor have I met a man like you, Mr. Nugent," I said in all honesty.

"Maybe you will let me escort you to Longmont."

"Yes, that would be most welcome."

"Weather can change here in a hurry. Usually, get an afternoon storm this time of year. It's a quick downpour and wont' hurt you none, but it's time to head back," he said gathering up our picnic.

On the ride home we spotted a wagon coming up the trail from Longmont. It was Evans! Mr. Nugent bid me farewell. I galloped down the mountain to greet Evans. I hoped for letters from dear Hennie, money to continue my tour, and some new boots.

"Welcome back, Mr. Evans. What good news have you?" I asked unable to contain my excitement.

"Sorry Miss Bird, I'm afraid good news is in short supply. The financial panic has spread out West. The Denver banks have all suspended business. They refuse to cash their own checks or to allow their customers to draw a dollar. They wouldn't even give greenbacks for English Gold."

"This is very bad news indeed. What of my boots?"

"Sorry ma'am. I couldn't get a red cent and had to make use of your money to get supplies and get back up here before the snow flies. I'm sorry. I can make it up to you with interest and room and board."

"What of letters?" I asked totally deflated.

"You didn't get any mail. I have to get these supplies to the lodge. I will see you there." With that he cracked the whip over the exhausted mules and went on.

Shocked at this disheartening news, I didn't know what made me sadder: no news from my sister or the fact that no matter how rich you were, at this moment you were poor. I was not certain what my next step would be.

Merriment returned to the lodge with Evans' arrival. He broke out his accordion and roused us to song with his inexhaustible repertoire, but I my heart was not in it. A cask filled with spirits was passed around increasing the raucousness of the festivities.

Evans announced that the Indians have taken to the war path again. "They been burning ranches and killing cattle. There is a scare among the settlers and wagon loads of fugitives are arriving in Colorado Springs."

"If the soldiers hadn't killed off the buffalo, they wouldn't be so angry," Nate said.

"Starvin' those redskins out is the only way to get rid of them for good," Evans replied.

"Anytime you put a man's back to the wall he's going to fight, no matter what color his skin is," Nate said.

This news did not bode well for my plan. Melancholy was setting in. Just then Mrs. Edwards came from the kitchen with a packet in her hand. "Miss Bird, look what I found in the groceries. Griff must have dropped it there and forgot about it."

Not all was lost! I tore the paper wrapping a stack of letters from Hennie. There was also an invitation from Miss Karpe to join her in Denver.

Dancing Bears

We were enjoying Evans' welcome home dinner with freshly baked bread, trout from the lake, and new potatoes when a shot rang out.

"Come out here Evans, you snake!" bellowed Mountain Jim.

Then two more shots rang out. "Get out here and take your punishment like a man."

Evans stood up, picked up his rifle "Get the children in the other room." Mrs. Edwards grabbed them by the shoulders and scurried them into the bed closet.

"Jim is in a fit ma'am. You better take cover," Nate said.

Evans opened the door and went out to meet his enemy. I knelt below the sill of the window overlooking the yard to see Mr. Nugent obviously drunk beyond reason with revolver in hand pointing it to the sky.

"You sold out, didn't you scum!" Enraged, Jim accused Evans of selling his land to Dunraven.

“Who told you that?” Evans said.

“You been helping Dunraven all along. Pretending to care about what happens here.”

“You are drunk again Jim. Put your gun down.”

“I’ll put my gun down if you will set your rifle aside.”

Evans knew Jim was so drunk he could easily out-fight him, so he took up the challenge. The moment Evans set his rifle on the ground Jim tackled him. Both were burly, brawny, heavy-set men about the same height. Evenly matched, they swirled in a clench like two dancing bears. Jim broke free and took a swing at Evans landing a solid punch that knocked him backwards. Evans, now angered, lunged at Jim and took him to the ground. He punched Jim in the face with all the force he could muster. Blood spurted from Jim’s nose. Jim managed to wriggle out from Evans’ girth and got to his feet. He took a boxing stance and stepped into Evans, landing punches in this mid-section that took Evans’ breath away. Evans was reaching for his rifle when another shot rang out. Both men stood stock still looking to see who had fired the shot.

Nate had a bead on both of them.

“Go home Jim. This isn’t going solve anything,” Nate said.

Evans got up and dusted himself off and said, "Put your gun down Nate."

"Ain't doin' that until both of you settle down."

Mr. Nugent put a bandana to his bloodied nose, picked up his revolver and glared at Evans. "This isn't over. You can't get away with this," he said, and left.

Now I had seen what Jim was like when he had one of his so-called fits. I waited a couple days before stopping by to share what I had written about our time on Longs Peak with him. Ring rushed to me wagging his tail. I patted his massive head as I trod among the bones and skulls strewn around the entrance to the cabin. I knocked lightly on Jim's door not knowing what sort of temper he would be in.

He peered at me from the gloomy depths of his den. "What brings you here Miss Bird?"

"I wanted to share a passage in my journal with you about our climb. May I come in?"

He opened the door exposing his muscular bare chest covered with a mat of champagne curls. "Come in, I will get dressed," he said grabbing a rawhide shirt from a nearby hook.

His cabin was in disarray with old magazines and books scattered on the wooden floor. A massive bear rug lay spread before the hearth and there was an elk head with giant rack hanging on the wall. Beaver, mink, and ermine pelts were lying about. I spied what looked like a writing desk. I couldn't smell spirits on his breath, and hoped his black spell was over.

His mood was dark and morose, but he behaved like a gentleman. "Have a seat by the fire. I will build it up for you."

I read my passage that was filled with exultation and gratitude for the privilege of having sat at God's pulpit. It ended with: "Uplifted above love and hate and storms of passion, calm amidst the eternal silences, fanned by zephyrs and bathed in living blue, peace rested for that one bright day on the Peak."

"I could not have known that peace without you," I said.

"Don't think anything of it. The least I could do for a lady in distress," he didn't say this with his usual disarming smile. He wasn't his congenial, gracious self. He was withdrawn almost sulking. I dared to broach the subject.

"What did Evans do that made you attack him?"

"He has been helping Dunraven with his scheme to buy up all the land around here. There is talk that he is making a deal with him to sell his land and the lodge to him."

"Do you really think you can stop the changes that are coming? Settlers are coming west in droves. Maybe his plan is not what you would like, but it might be better than a patchwork of ramshackle homesteads like what I saw on the plains."

At first, he didn't respond. Then, bleary eyed, he began a story of inconceivable horror.

"I have been trapping in these mountains since I was a young lad. My best friend was a Cheyanne named Running Deer. He taught me everything I know about hunting and tracking and a lot more about life. He belonged to Black Kettle's tribe. They were good people who lived here in peace. When the civil war was ending, the army turned its attention to eradicating the Indian people. Nothing short of extermination would please them. I got hooked up in being part of the infantry that was assigned to relocate Black Kettle's village.

"It was all a lie. They were not planning on relocating The People. Col. Chivington fired up his men to kill every woman and child in the sleeping village at Sand Creek. They rained down their terror taking no prisoners, hacking up their victims, taking body parts for trophies. I saw a soldier chase down the most beautiful woman I have ever known. She was an angel of mercy who nursed me after my tangle with the bear that ripped my face. He shot her in the back then rolled her over and ripped open her belly." He stopped, overcome with emotion. "What happened next is too wretched for a lady's tender sensibilities."

He paused, gazing into the fire.

"But I did nothing. I did nothing to stop what was happening. I betrayed my brother. I ran like a coward and did nothing to save his squaw, Shining Moon."

He stopped and gathered himself and looked at me with an intense ice-blue eye, "I can't just do nothing now. I have to try to stop the mountains from being raped by men who slaughter for sport leaving carcasses to rot. Men who killed off the buffalo so the Indian people would starve. Men who have broken all their promises to good people. I have to do something to check their greed and grasping nature. I have to save the wild."

I fell silent not certain how I should respond to the fate of a ruined man. Wretched with guilt. Derelict from drink.

"Mr. Nugent, I pray you will curb the tide that is quickly rising around you."

After a moment, I dared to continue.

"May I say that drink will not help you? I once was dependent upon laudanum to bear the pain that would not let go of my body. It lifted me from the melancholy I could not override and allowed me to sleep. It was on this journey that I have finally become whole and no longer need a drug to roll back my depression. You helped me with that. That is what I wanted to tell you. You gave me the strength to persevere."

At this he crumbled and laid his head in my lap and sobbed. His broad shoulders heaved with unchecked emotion. I fondled his blonde curls and rubbed his head tenderly.

He recovered himself and said, "You have come to me too late. I am lost, lost, lost. Unredeemable. A wreck of man."

I lifted the face of this desperado and wiped the tears from his cheek. He began to unbutton my blouse. I did not stop him. He kissed my nipples, sucking on them sweetly. His gaze fell on the purple welts beneath my breasts left from the metal brace I wore for two years.

He looked up and I met his gaze. He was the first witness to my suffering. I felt it time for him to know my story. "When I was a child of ten it was determined that the cause of constant pain in my spine was a tumor. Various combinations of medicines to reduce the pain were administered to no avail. Finally, six years later, I was operated on without anesthesia. My screams of terror went unheeded as electric currents of pain sluiced through my body. The wound was not cauterized, and infection set in. Many applications of burning medications like acid in veins settled into dull pain. I grew inward in my suffering which only became more intense as years went by. A well-meaning surgeon created an iron brace that enveloped my core to help my weakened spine. It did not help. Finally, the doctor suggested I go on sea voyage around the world to take my mind off what he deemed an incurable situation. Amazingly on this tour I have regained my strength. I couldn't let you know my frailty for fear you would not take me to the summit."

An errant tear rolled down my cheek as he guided me down to the bear rug before the fire. His tender affections were intoxicating. I was lost. Lost to his savaged beauty and tortured heart.

The next day, I sat beside Mirror Lake holding my knees and rocking back and forth contemplating my rippled reflection. Feeling precious and fragile after a night of lovemaking, I smiled to myself. I had no desire for children but had yearned to know the depths of my own sensuality. My father had spun a sticky web of his own guilt around me forming a chrysalis that encapsulated me in morbid melancholy. I felt anger and resentment rising.

Like an afternoon storm, the dark clouds of my emotions swarmed forming a gray shroud over majestic Longs Peak. A shuddering sob rose from my belly and overtook me. Tears streamed uncontrollably and a howl as savage as that of any wolf rose from my throat calling out the God that had condemned me to an island of solitude. A crashing jolt of recognition like the jagged bolts that light the sky ripped through me.

Then, like the brilliant sun breaking through the gray revealing a tender blue sky as clear and sweet as the breath of a newborn, my mind was freed. It came clear. Years lost to lassitude, shackled by the expectations of others, at the mercy of well-meaning but ignorant physicians, was over. Never more would I follow anyone's path but one of my own making. I wiped the tears from my cheeks with the back of my hand, stood up, dusted off my bottom and saw a self-possessed woman standing before me in the translucent water.

Taste of Society

It was difficult to tear myself away from the freedoms and enchantment of my cabin in Estes Park, but winter was upon me. My pre-arranged mountain tour was a now-or-never proposition. The original plan was to be touring in the summer, but my extended stay in the Islands meant riding in November. The day broke clear beneath tender blue skies. I packed my bag and strapped it behind my saddle. Birdie, full of high spirits, was as eager as I for an adventure. We galloped the four miles to Muggin's Gulch to meet up with Mr. Nugent who determined that he should escort me to Longmont.

The trail along the St. Vrain was never more beautiful. Snow piled in the gloom of narrow, dark rock gorges. Birdie is such a little beauty—fast, enduring, gentle, and wise. She stepped smartly through it all. I bid silent farewell to the snowclad peaks glistening in the morning sun.

When we reached my lodgings in Longmont,

Mr. Nugent gave me a gift I was not certain I wanted.

"I don't see a weapon in your kit. Here, take this. You might need it." He handed me a small packet. Inside was a derringer with a supply of ammunition.

"I have never used a gun," I said.

"I hope you don't have to use one, but you could run into highwaymen, or worse. It is not good for a lady to be traveling alone."

I thanked him but felt certain I would not have to use a weapon. My greater concern was running out of money. The banks were still closed and not honoring my notes. I was counting on the legendary hospitality in the West.

With that, he leaned over and gave me a sweet kiss of farewell. "I'll be thinking of you out there in the world," he said as he tipped his beaver hat. "Safe journey Miss Bird." And with that he turned his horse and galloped back up the trail to his mountain home.

I felt forlorn at his departure but was determined to keep my promises to myself. It is a dreary ride of thirty miles across brown plains to Denver. It felt like I was embarking on an ocean voyage without a compass. I was told to steer south, but trails meandered in all directions. I met a traveler every mile or so in this vast emptiness.

By noon storm clouds had gathered and a black gloom was settling in with a fierce cold wind. I met a parade of prairie schooners filled with immigrants laboring their way to what they hoped would be a new life in the West. One woman invited me to rest with them. She told of the horrors they had endured thus far in their exodus from the East. Attacks by wild savages, the death of her first born to disease, the pestilence of insects, but still she had good cheer.

The windy cold became intense as I raced to get to Denver before the full force of the storm was unleashed. I could see the "Metropolis of the Territories" spread out on a brown, treeless plain fed by the shriveled Platte River. Then a dust storm obscured the view of the town altogether. I arrived at dusk and asked a good citizen for directions to the address Miss Karpe had given me. A rose-covered arbor opened the pathway to her stately Victorian home on the edge of town. I was relieved to see Miss Karpe herself opening the door when I rang the bell.

"Isabella, you made it!" She gushed with genuine excitement so freely expressed by Americans. She gave me a welcoming hug and scurried me into the parlor.

"Come in and get comfortable. You must be exhausted from your long ride. Our stable hand will attend to your horse." She took my bag and led me up a spiral staircase to a gracious bedroom with lace curtains, a fireplace, and four-poster bed.

"I've been so worried about you out there traveling alone," she said.

"Yes, well I admit there have been moments that made me question my purpose."

"I want to hear all about it," she said with eager anticipation.

"Get freshened up. I will tell Hannah to set another plate at the table. Dinner is at seven," she said leaving me to enjoy the comforts of her home.

I have to admit, the trappings of civilization were most welcome. I drew a bath and soaked for an hour giving my aching muscles a rest. I sank into the down feather mattress beneath the canopy and took a proper snooze before dinner. I changed into the simple black dress I had somehow preserved on my journey and went down to dinner.

To my surprise Miss K had invited guests all who were eager to hear of my escapades.

She was wearing an elegant off-the-shoulder emerald silk dress that matched the color of her eyes. The polished oak table was set with fine china, silver, and gleaming candelabras.

"Isabella, may I introduce you to our Governor Hunt and his wife Sarah, Earl Dunraven, and my father Charles."

"Welcome to Denver, Miss Bird. We understand you are on a grand tour of our territory," said the governor extending a welcoming hand in greeting.

"It is a pleasure to meet such a daring traveler," said Earl Dunraven, wearing a tweed hunt coat that identified him as a "High Toner." He bowed and lightly kissed the back of my hand.

"Such a pleasure to meet you Miss Bird. My daughter has told us of her wild ride with you on the flank of the volcano in Hawai'i," said Mr. Karpe.

I hadn't missed the comforts of civilization, but it was a pleasure to be in gentle company. Hannah, the hired girl, served a salad to start, followed by a prime rib entrée, and apple pie for dessert.

"So, what of your stay so far? Has it met your expectations?" the governor asked.

"Yes, the glories of the Rockies are unsurpassed. I had only one rude encounter when I gave my trust over to a buffoon named Chalmers. He took me on wild goose chase that ended in disaster. He told me he knew the way to Estes Park, but proceeded in taking on a trail where my horse fell and I nearly landed in the gorge carved by the Big Thompson River."

"How dreadful for you!" exclaimed Miss Karpe.

“You must have encountered Rocky Mountain Jim, the self-proclaimed ‘Guardian of the Mountains,’ when you did reach Estes Park,” Dunraven said.

“Yes, I did make his acquaintance.”

“He is loved by many people in the territory who don’t want to see change. Every month there is an editorial about him, or one that he has written in the *Gazette*. He has caused quite a furor,” Mr. Karpe said dabbing his mouth with his napkin.

“Lord Dunraven is working towards bringing a more sophisticated tourist to the beauty of our region. We have thousands of consumptives and asthmatics here for the cure, but we want a more affluent tourist to build our city,” Governor Hunt said.

“Thank you, Governor. I’m glad you see my vision as a good one,” Earl Dunraven said. “I will be honest with you, Miss Bird. I know you will be writing about your mountain tour and I would like you to know my side of the story. I have invested a great percentage of my wealth into procuring land that will be used as a retreat for wealthy Europeans and Easterners. It will re-create the hunts with horses and hounds in your homeland. I am building a hotel as magnificent as any in England with all the amenities for equestrians and hunters alike. There will be trophy hunters, equestrians, and fisherman from all over the world who will pay to experience the magnificence of my mountain retreat."

"I didn't realize there is such a divide over Mr. Nugent's calling to protect the mountains from the encroachments of civilization," I lied. "Without him, I would not have been able to reach my goal of summiting Longs Peak."

"I hope you haven't become smitten with him, Isabella," Miss K said with a knowing smile.

"How could I be charmed by such a rash and careless man? I am only saying that without his help, I could not have known the majesty of his realm."

Desperately wanting to change the subject, I addressed Earl Dunraven. "Is it true, sir, that you were with Stanley on his expedition in Africa?"

"Why yes, madam, it was a venture that changed my life. The Dark Continent is of endless fascination but is not a place I should choose to live. The beauty of this wild place holds a great deal more charm for me. How did you know about my past?"

"I am not the only one here with notoriety that precedes them," I said.

"I admire your pluck Miss Bird. Not many women choose to tour our mountains alone, certainly not in winter. I look forward to reading what you have to say about the youngest state in the Union," Mrs. Hunt said.

I hoped the dinner would end soon. I didn't like the thought of having my words manipulated. My journals are self-reflection, not fodder for political ambitions. It was obvious they hoped to gain my support. They did not know I would be the last to encourage taming of the wild.

"May I see the detail of your itinerary? I can craft a letter of letter of introduction to potential hosts along the way," Governor Hunt offered.

"Why, that would be most kind. With funds unavailable, I will have to stretch what I have on hand to the limit."

"We want you to know you are welcome here should you pass through Denver again," Mr. Karpe said.

"Let me show you Denver before your leave us," insisted Miss K.

Denver, home to 16,000 hardy souls is a dusty hub of commerce with a striking view of the Rocky Range. A menagerie of the western denizens gather here for supplies. Hunters come for ammunitions, rifles, and supplies for month-long stays in the mountains. Settlers in long lines of covered wagons refresh their larders for the next leg of their journey West. Gold miners in bedraggled condition line up at the assayer's office with their hard-won findings. Hollow-eyed Indians wearing blankets over their shoulders sit cross-legged in front of the Indian agency waiting for dispensation. It saddened me to see a once proud, independent race reduced to handouts. Cattlemen wearing high-heeled boots and broad-brimmed hats are here to get the best price for beef they herded for hundreds of miles. Consumptives gather here in the hundreds seeking the cure in the dry air. Many of them are outfitted here in Denver with camp gear and supplies for camping in the summer. In the winter, they return and fill the hotels to capacity. They even hold an asthmatic convention each year.

"That is where your friend Mountain Jim got into a brawl with Comanche Bill. The sheriff had to be called out to keep them from killing one another. They both had to spend a night in jail," Miss K informed me as we passed by the Last Chance Saloon where men were bellied up to the bar before noon. Ladies of negotiable affections sat in the swing on the porch fanning themselves in the bright morning sun.

Women in stylish frocks strolled arm in arm on the planks lining the shops with wooden façades. Men walked the streets with revolvers in their belts, some wearing blue cloaks, relics of the civil war. There were English dandies sporting kid gloves and knee-high riding boots. Even though I appreciated the respite with Miss K in Denver, I was eager to get on with my journey. I wearied of the bustle of the city and the expectations of my gracious hosts. I yearned to be back in the solemn purity of the mountains.

Mountain Tour

It was a lovely Indian summer day on the plains when I mounted Birdie. As usual, the gallant pony appeared as eager as I to get on the road. All traces of snow had melted in the warm sun. Fresh from the week off, she galloped across the plain as though she enjoyed it. The first day out was a great pleasure. I yearned for the solitude that allows my thoughts to settle. Riding alone encourages introspection. The rhythmic sound of Birdie's hoof beats and the puffing of her warm breath sent me into a quiet meditation. Time with my dear desperado had changed me and filled me with unanswered questions. Could I now continue to live without the tender attentions of a loving man as I had done for the first forty years of my life? Would I become incurably bored without society and find a man to be another entrapment? Should I go on with my journey, or should I stop here in the heartbeat of the wild? It is in the interludes between being in company that we talk to ourselves. In the silence we listen to ourselves. In the quietude we find answers.

It is the custom of the West to take travelers in, as there are no hotels, and the weather can be fearsome. On the first night out, I saw a light burning in the window of a tidy log cabin with a grey stream of smoke rising from its chimney. A plump woman with rosy cheeks opened the door and bid me welcome. I slept with her children that night. When approaching settlers for lodging, sometimes I was only offered a mat on the floor and a biscuit for breakfast. After a week of riding ten hours a day staying at the homes of good people who opened their homes to me, I arrived at the home of Mr. Perry. Here my letter of introduction from Governor Hunt provided me comfort at his elegant farmhouse. Mr. Perry is a millionaire twice over from his cattle ranch. Here I enjoyed stewed venison and various other luxuries including hot water and a feather bed.

"You must let me take you to Pleasant Park, Miss Bird. It offers some of the finest scenery in the territory," Mr. Perry's daughter Lilah insisted.

"I would relish the opportunity to have you as a guide. Thank you."

Miss Perry led the way to the narrow pass guarded by two bright red upright buttes. A remarkable display of monumental rocks standing in shocking colors of vermillion and orange framed the gorge carved by Bear Creek. Lilah said the cliffs lining the gorge reminded her of scenes in Egypt where she had a traveled with her family.

That night a storm arrived dropping a foot of snow. Birdie and I set out early while the sun was creeping over the horizon. I wanted to make it to the Arkansas Divide before nightfall. The world was silent, buried underneath a glittering carpet of white. The thin limbs of the birch stripped of leaves bent in the chill wind. There is purity mixed with solemnity in winter. No one had passed this way so there were no tracks to tell us if we were going in the right direction. No birds sang, no branches creaked. It was absolutely eerie. The only sound was the crunch of snow under Birdie's hooves. We came to a bridge on a creek bound in ice. Birdie balked, which was so not like her. I urged her forward, but she reared and would not be swayed. Finally, she chose to enter the creek itself, but would not step foot on the bridge. Later, I learned the bridge was dangerous. I have come to love this pony with wild horse blood.

We ascended in silence and loneliness toward the Continental Divide at 7,975 feet. I stopped when we reached a cabin near a frozen lake. By nightfall, the temperature had dropped to below zero. A fierce wind whipped the pines. I was nearly paralyzed with the cold and my feet were frozen to the wooden stirrup. Two German ladies who lived in this desolate place boiled water and massaged my feet that were stinging with a thousand needles. My room was reached by a ladder. There were seventeen snowbound men lying on the floor of the main hall. No one is turned away in a storm.

The sun shone brightly the next day even though the air was still crackling. I am the lone tourist here and it suits me fine for I have had enough of company. One of the most wonderful things about traveling alone is that you can go at your own pace—the exact speed that makes you comfortable. You can stop serendipitously to marvel at what incites your imagination. After twelve miles, I entered a wild, romantic glen I thought must be Glen Eyrie. Encased in ghastly peaks, it offered wild and inspiring scenery. I drank in the healing beauty. Thoreau spoke of this in his essay on the benefits of solitude: "To live fully in the world our aspiration should be to absorb the continuity of nature not to attempt to dominate it."

My letter of introduction provided safe harbor at General Palmer's baronial mansion. Its fine hall was lined with mounted buffalo, elk, and deer heads. This was to be my last taste of luxury on the tour.

Next, I entered bleak, treeless Colorado Springs scattered with plain wooden houses. I found lodging in a boarding house filled with guests. Through a half-open door, I saw two white feet dangling out from the covers in one of the bedrooms. In the morning I learned the feet belonged to a man who was consumptive. He had passed in the night and was to be buried in the morning. Had I known this I think I would have preferred sleeping in the stable with Birdie.

Armed with a warm coat and gloves, I set off on Birdie for Manitou hot springs, long known to the Indians to be healing. Thousands of consumptives come here in the summer to drink the waters and enjoy mountain excursions, but it is all quiet now. Snowclad peaks that rise to 14,500 feet overhang the valley slashed by a rushing torrent. It is grand and awful in its menacing beauty. I hope to get to Ute Pass by tomorrow, but all may be lost as Birdie has thrown a shoe. She amuses everyone we meet with her affections for me. She walks after me, lays her head on my shoulder teasing me for sugar. Luckily, we found a blacksmith and were able to reach Ute Pass by nightfall.

Ute Pass lies in the shadow of pine-sheathed mountains. A torrent blasted out the river corridor. A narrow track overlooking the ravine went ever higher for twenty miles. The stream cuts through hard rocks and tumbles over rose-red granite. It is a cold, dark, arduous climb. Above the towering cliffs, toothy snowclad peaks glitter in the morning sun. It was grand and glorious, but not lovable like Hawai'i. At that moment I yearned for the warm breezes and luxuriant foliage of the Islands.

I found shelter at a settler's home and slept soundly after the arduous ride. There was not a cloud in the sky when I awoke next morning. This is an amazing climate with blazing sun by day and below-zero temperatures at night. The creeks crackle in the day, breaking through the ice formed at night. Waterfalls are frozen shafts of diamonds. The trees grew shorter, and the shrubs hugged the ground as we climbed toward the Divide.

I reached Bergen's Park touted to rival Estes Park in beauty, but it made me miss my mountain home even more. The higher we climbed the more snow lay piled on the ground. The track was hard to see and often I had to rely on Birdie's keen sense. By midday, we were tromping through snow up to her belly. She slipped and fell into a drift and struggled to free herself. I got off to help her recover and sank into the snow up to my shoulders! Damp and dis-spirited, we managed to slog on until we reached Colonel Kittridge's cabin at Oil Creek where we spent the night with agreeable people.

I awoke to another cloudless morning feeling

refreshed and ready to enjoy the demands of another day. I saw a man riding about a mile ahead of me and rode to overtake him. I requested his company as he knew the track and I had become lonely on my solitary ride. He was a most congenial, charming companion. He wore a big slouch hat under which curls hung to his waist. His beard was fair, his eyes blue, and his complexion ruddy. He dressed in a hunter's buckskin suit and jangled a huge pair of Mexican spurs. His saddle was ornamented with silver amulets. He carried a rifle across his saddle, a pair of pistols holsters, two revolvers, knife in his belt, and a carbine slung behind him. He was full of stories about his hunting adventures. I rode with him across South Park to Breckenridge Pass. When we reached the Great Divide, he escorted me to a cabin where I could find lodging for the night.

"I'm sure you enjoyed the company of Comanche Bill. He is a real gentleman," the kindly woman who lived in the cabin informed me. It turned out my courteous companion was a notorious desperado and the greatest Indian exterminator on the frontier. "His family fell in a massacre at Spirit Lake by the hands of the Indians who carried away his eleven-year-old sister. His life has since been devoted to killing Indians wherever he finds them," she said.

Now, I understood why Mr. Nugent and this otherwise charming murderer would be at odds. Jim was a defender of the Indians and Comanche Bill was determined to exterminate them. Still, this did not excuse outrageous behavior.

The talk between my hostess and two Irish ladies was about a lynching that took place the day before I arrived. They pointed to a tree on a distant knoll where the wretch had met his end. He had been tried, convicted, and strung up all within an hour's time. Their tales were filled with grisly, cruel acts. This country is untamed. Busted miners, hunters, and criminals hiding from the law find refuge in the high country.

The Great Divide, the goal of my journey, was disappointing. Lonely, mournful, treeless, and windswept, its chief center was a rough mining town ironically dubbed Fairplay. The region has been "rushed" and mining camps sprung up here are so lawless and brutal that vigilantes take matters into their own hands. I slept with the derringer Jim had given me beneath my pillow that night.

I struck out the next morning for the Denver Stage Road that would take me back to Denver. I hoped that would end my rough passage, but it turned out to be the rudest, darkest route yet. It took me through a ravine walled in on both sides by pine clad mountains. For fifty miles along this abyss, there are only five houses. My energies were flagging. I left a silent, dreary sea of white only to descend into this hellish ravine. Snow in the shadow of the mountains didn't melt, rather it piled up into huge drifts. Birdie kept falling on her nose because the snow balled up in her feet. I didn't have a pick strong enough to free her from slipping and sliding downhill. I had to dismount and walk with her through deep drifts.

It was totally black out when at last I saw the blaze of a hunter's fire. They directed me to a cabin nearby. A man of good nature who was obviously intoxicated opened the door to the smoke-filled den. There were other snowbound travelers lying about that included an English dandy, a couple of miners, and a hunter who appeared to be in a fever. They asked me if I was the English lady written about in the *Denver News*. For once I was glad my reputation preceded me. I opted to sleep in a shed with my derringer under my pillow than inside the lair of these rough men.

I was ready for my tour to end, but I had many miles to go before reaching Denver. Birdie, "Queen of Ponies," and I had traveled nearly six hundred miles. Even though the scenery was awe-inspiring, it paled to the view from my cabin window in Estes Park of Longs Peak, the King of the Rocky Range.

In fairness, I was traveling in November which is not the optimum time to visit alpine regions, but winter has a silent, serene beauty of its own. With only 26 cents and my letter of introduction in my pocket, I was running out of options. I determined to skip a few stops on my itinerary and head directly to Evans homestead on the plains. If the banks were still not open, I hoped to retrieve the $100 I had given him.

Winter's Grip

When I reached the Evans homestead their teen daughter ran towards me, but she had not come to welcome me, it was Birdie she was so excited to see. I was happy to turn the tired pony over to her for grooming. Evans had just returned from Estes Park with three elk, one grizzly, and one bighorn sheep in his wagon. Their welcoming home smelled of bread baking in the oven.

"Miss Bird, we were getting worried about you," said Mrs. Evans who came from the kitchen wiping her hands on her apron to greet me.

"Yes, we were afraid you got snowed in up on the Divide, but sure enough looks like you made it," Griff said, giving me a hug that nearly lifted me off my feet. His jovial manner did not quell my fear that he still did not have my money. I took him aside and asked him plainly,

"Have you my $100 so that I may purchase a train ticket to New York?"

"No ma' am. I don't. Nothing has changed. The

banks are still closed. I have a family and livestock to feed. But you can stay at the cabin in Estes until the banks open. I am sorry, but all I can give you is room and board in exchange for helping out Nate and the Edwards up there. I will give you your money when I can."

It wasn't the answer I wanted, but it was one I could live with. I didn't mind being a hired girl for a while as long as I wasn't asked to bake bread!

When I arrived at Muggin's Gulch, I was disappointed that Ring did not charge out to meet me and there was no sign of Mr. Nugent. Snow was piled around his cabin and it looked cold and forlorn. At Evans Lodge I learned that the Edwards family left the day before for their home on the plains. I was to share my time with Nate and two young men. Jack and Tracy from Longmont were in need of work and Evans had hired them to help Nate tend to the stock.

"Will Mr. Nugent be back?" I asked Nate, trying to hide my eagerness for his return.

"Yes, ma'am, but didn't say when. He left in a black mood saying he was headed for the Snowy Range. Said he needed to think things through."

I was even more disheartened to see my cabin boarded up for the winter. I truly loved my solitude there. I was sad that I had missed the

Edwards departure. I was to stay in the lodge with the men. The main hall was in general disarray with guns, saddles, and other tack lying about. It smelled of stale pipe smoke and there were dishes left on the table. They had been “bachin” it. With Mrs. Edwards gone, the nearest woman was twenty-five miles away. The men eyed me with disdain, afraid that my presence would put an end to their lazy comforts.

I assured them I would be happy to help with chores, but that I was no good at baking bread. Luckily, it turned out that Nate was an excellent baker who produced the best sourdough bread I have ever eaten. However, food in general was in short supply. The chickens were only laying one egg a day and the cows were not delivering milk. Pickled pork was our mainstay, and we had to ration what we had of that until Evans returned with needed provisions.

Still, nothing I had seen on my tour of Colorado rivals Estes Park. I was delighted to be back. The peaks glittered in the distance. Pine boughs laden with snow were dazzling in the noon day sun. Though severe in winter, there is nothing more sublime than the heart of the inner world. The healing air, pure water, and absolute dryness are life giving. Unlike the damp, wet snow of Scotland that chills to the bone, the snowflakes here are light and fluffy. The isolation is intense, but welcome. Winter provides a rest for the bears, bees, marmots, and other creatures who hibernate. The elk and deer do not hibernate, but they slow down. Even trees go dormant. I found myself sleeping into shameful hours and bedding early. After my taxing mountain tour, nature provided me with a winter's nap.

I am kept busy sweeping and cleaning dishes. Tracy and Jack have learned that I am a most agreeable person and have come to enjoy my company. We sit about in the evenings by the fire telling stories. I write my letters to Hennie while they oil their rifles and clean tack. Nate kept my ink well on the kitchen stove to keep it from freezing. We were down to rationing food to two meals a day. I couldn't swallow any more pickled pork, so Tracy cut a hole in the ice on the lake and caught us a string of trout for dinner. Jack went hunting and bagged an elk he planned to sell in Longmont, but we were so starving he cut steaks for us. No meat ever tasted so good.

A threatening dark cover of clouds settled over our hidden world. The wind howled along with the wolves outside who had taken down a deer, or an elk. The demonic noise they made snarling over the carcass of the sorry beast haunts me. I woke next morning with frost on my eyelashes, a blanket of snow on my cover and snow an inch thick on the floor. The storm that had come in over the night remained for two days. Still, no Evans. I feared we would be snowed in for the winter without enough food.

That night, Nate answered a knock at the door.

"Come on in Brother. Get out of the weather and sit yourself by the fire," I heard him say.

It was Mr. Nugent and Ring back from the Snowy Mountains. He stomped the snow off his moccasins and brushed flakes from the wolf skin ruff framing his face. Ring shook himself sending a misty spray in the air then settled himself by the fire. Jim seemed subdued, but not angry or nearing one of his fits.

Nate left the room to tend to his cooking.

"I found Birdie pinned in a ravine," Jim said. "Thought you might like to have her back. I put her in the stable."

Birdie had broken loose and wandered off with a couple of other horses. I had not been able to look after her in the storm. I worried she'd been taken down by wolves.

"It is time for me to thank you again," I said, grateful he had rescued the Queen of Ponies.

Jim took off his jacket and hat freeing his curls. His manner was calm, almost submissive. He took my hand in his.

"I haven't had a drink for the whole time I was in the Snowy Range," he announced.

"And how has that been for you?" I asked, knowing from my charitable work in the church how hard it is for wretched souls addicted to drink to hold their resolve.

"Difficult. Drink is a part of my dereliction, but not the root of it. Still, I had become accustomed to the numbness it provides."

"And, what of your mountain tour? Did you find it worthwhile?" he asked, moving away from the subject of his dependency on drink.

"It held its charms, and the solitude was most welcome, but in truth I find Estes Park most fair and the grandeur of Longs Peak unrivaled."

"I know you love the mountains in the way that I do," he said, clearing his throat looking deeply into my eyes searching for confirmation. I sensed he was about to say something we would both regret.

"I think I could make you happy if you would…." I put my finger to his lips and stopped him from going further and asking the obvious question.

"We are wed in spirit. I have nothing but love for you in my heart, but my course is set." I did not want to say it and was not sure I was giving the right answer, but I continued: "My passage to

England was booked before I arrived. I must get to Denver to catch the train to New York."

He stepped back pained at my revelation. Abject despair held him frozen. I have never seen a man with such a disheartened look of betrayal. He turned away from me. It took a moment for him to pull his emotions into check and to digest this rejection. I was afraid I had sent him hurtling back into the solace of the bottle. He gathered himself then turned back to me and flashed a disarming smile.

Madam, if that is your final decision, may I at least escort you to Denver?"

"Your company would be most welcome, Mr. Nugent. I ride in the morning."

He donned his beaver hat and left leaving me wondering if I had done the right thing. I believed that if I stayed, my love would turn to bitterness and resentment towards him. I also did not trust his resolve for sobriety. He had a genius and special gifts that could be redeemed, but would they be? We both found sustenance and solace in nature, but I could not be confined. It was my time to escape from the tyranny of trying to fit into the mold of others.

It was a lonely, mournful ride out of Estes Park, but when we entered the beautiful canyon of the St. Vrain the sun rose brilliant, warm, and scintillating. By now I knew the curves of the valley and tried to blaze this most gorgeous ride into my memory for safekeeping. When I arrived here in September, the valley floor was tangled in gay scarlet and gold vines. Now, it was barren, with patches of snow framed in the fantastically stained walls of rock.

We encountered Evans in his fully loaded wagon finally returning with supplies. Jim skirted Evans and kept riding without acknowledging him, but I stopped to talk.

"Miss Bird, I see you have heard the banks are open."

"No, I had not, but it is glad tidings you bear."

He reached inside his vest and pulled out his wallet. "Here is your $100. I hope the interest earned in room and board is a fair settlement."

"Yes, to be beauty bound is more than enough payment for me. Thank you."

"I best be getting on," he said, snapping his whip on the lathered rump of his mules.

"The boys will be glad to see you," I waved in farewell.

By the time we reached Longmont, Mr. Nugent had regained his sparkle. He led us on a merry romp across the barren plains on the way to Denver. We galloped side by side in the invigorating air until our ponies were puffing. He slowed to a walk and we talked as friends will do on a long trail ride.

"You are the first man or woman who's treated me like a human being for many a year," he said without any note of melancholy.

"I'm sure that's not true. There are many who agree with your cause."

"Feels good to wake up with a clear head," he announced.

"Does that mean you are re-claiming your life?"

"I don't know if I can, but I want to try."

"I'm afraid for you Mr. Nugent. I've heard talk. There are forces mounting against you. You could come with me. It's a big world and I'm going to see it."

"That's a pleasant prospect Miss Bird, but then who would be the Guardian of the Mountains? He laughed and urged his mare into a lope, and we were off again.

He deposited me at Miss K's home. She raised both eyebrows when she saw Jim at her doorstep.

"Would you like to come in Mr. Nugent, or is it Rocky Mountain Jim?" she offered with a flirtatious smile.

"No madam, thank you. I'm not used to such comforts," he said with a slight tip of his beaver hat.

I walked with him to the rail where our horses

were tied. I gave Birdie one last scratch under the chin and kissed her soft gray nose. She lay her head on my shoulder and fairly purred at my attentions. My Queen of Ponies had taken me 800 miles over perilous tracks, fording streams, through snow drifts and daunting ravines. Never once did she refuse my commands except for the icy, danger-ridden bridge.

I handed her reins to Mr. Nugent. “Please take good care of her. She has legs of steel and the heart of a tiger,” I said wincing back tears.

“She will be well tended,” he said leaning down to plant a whisper-soft kiss on my forehead.

“I know we will meet in again in the by and by,” he said.

He mounted his own regal mare, and with Birdie in tow, spurred into a gallop towards the splendid isolation of his mountain home.

I waved him farewell and prayed my fears for my dear desperado would not find fruition.

Epilogue

Six months later while sleeping in a bed in Switzerland, I was awakened by a vivid dream in which I saw Mr. Nugent. I jolted upright knowing something had happened to him. It brought back his premonition that we would meet again in the sweet by and by. I contacted Miss Karpe and she confirmed what I knew in my heart. She told me that Mr. Nugent was passing by Evans Lodge when he was shot without any provocation. It is rumored Lord Dunraven was inside the lodge at the time and that he encouraged Griff Evans to open fire on Jim. The tragedy that followed is too painful to dwell upon. Jim lived for several months after the initial attempt on his life. He wrote this statement that was published in the *Fort Collins Standard* on August 12, 1874.

> *It would seem that an all-wise providence has spared my life; that a hell-born plot to deprive a man of his life might be exposed.*

Justice is sometimes tardy, and the red-handed assassin and highway murderer oftimes escape the gallows and the prison cell. Sometimes by successful escape; sometimes by resort to gold. ....On the 10th day of June 1874, while riding peacefully along a highway in the company with one William Brown, when near the residence of one Griffith Evans, he approached me with a double barreled shotgun in his hands, and when within a few steps, without warning, raised his gun and fired, killing the horse I was riding and inflicting wound upon my person which fell me to the earth, and after I had fallen he deliberately walked up and shot me again through the head, turned upon his heel and disappeared into the house without even inquiry whether I was dead.

Jim's indictment of Evans continues. He hoped it would serve to bring him to justice, but the case never reached a tribunal. Brown was paid to leave so he would not testify. Some say Evans shot Jim because he had a dalliance with his daughter. Nothing was proven, but old timers say it is English Gold that killed Jim Nugent.

In later years, I learned that Dunraven's

scheme failed. The ill will brought about by the scandalous murder of Mr. Nugent caused locals to stop co-operating in his land acquisitions. The talk that he had fenced-in land claimed by illegal means finally led to a bold legal contest that drove him out of the region. Mr. Nugent's death was the catalyst that brought victory against the changes coming to the majestic peaks he loved so well.

I recall our rides in the Rocky Mountains together where we saw no man and were silent, listening to whispers of the wild. We were true children of the natural world then, and I remember him smiling tenderly at me and saying, "Once you've been in the mountains, they become a part of you, like the kiss of a lover."

Isabella Lucy Bird
Later Years

Isabella's travels did not end in Colorado. With an unlikely blend of frailty and ferocity, she ventured to the western edge of China where she was chased by people who had never seen a white woman before. She traveled by horseback, mule, and yak; rafted down raging Chinese rivers; traversed snow-blocked Tibetan mountains passes; and continued to the deserts of Morocco and the Middle East. She also explored Korea, Morocco, Viet Nam, and the humid forests of Malaysia.

In 1881, at the age of fifty-five, she married Dr. John Bishop, a man in his 30s. They traveled in Asia together, but within five years he died. She was left with a large inheritance that allowed her to continue her travels. In 1888, she was slowed down by a bout of scarlet fever but was not derailed completely.

At sixty, she went to India and on to Persia, Kurdistan, and Turkey. Featured articles of her travels and journals made her a household name back home in England. She became a photography buff and strapped her camera to her traveling chair. She never lost the desire instilled in her by her Evangelical father to serve others less fortunate. In India, she built the John Bishop Hospital with money allocated for that purpose in her husband's will.

Six Months in the Sandwich Islands was published in 1875 and received popular acclaim. Her fourth book, *A Lady in the Rockies*, is her most widely read narrative. The *Collected Works of Isabella Bird* provides excerpts from articles about her many exploits in what were unexplored regions at the time of her visit.

In 1891, she became the first woman to be elected a Fellow to the Scottish Royal Geographical Society. Well-deserved recognition for an extraordinary woman ahead of her time.

About the Author

A love triangle of extremes has proven to be a solid base for my writing. My turbulent teen years in southeastern Alaska connected me to the natural world. Long walks in the moody Tongass rainforest provided sustenance and solace and nurtured a love for the outdoors. That nature can be our salvation has become an abiding theme that runs throughout all my work. From Alaska, I journeyed to proud California where I obtained a degree in English literature and a doctorate in urban savvy. At twenty-eight, I dropped out of society for one year and landed on the north shore of Kauai where I found inspiration for my novel *Wai-nani, A Voice from Old Hawai'i.*

Like many parents, I can't help favoring my first born. The character of Wai-nani sprang from the dynamic life of Ka'ahumanu, the favorite wife of Kamehameha the Great. A brave, athletic, strong-willed, sensual being, she embodied the empowered woman. Researching for the book became a beautiful obsession that lasted several decades. Being true to the culture became my greatest challenge, and the result of my effort remains my proudest achievement.

Back in California I immersed myself in the horse world. An injury forced me to give up my mare and the life I loved. Writing *The Cowgirl Jumped Over the Moon* was part of my healing process. It allowed me to fulfill my riding aspirations, to let go and move on to my next chapter—adventure travel writing. Now, if I am not hiking, river rafting, taking horse treks, or globetrotting, I am writing about my experiences.

Lost Angel Walkabout is a spirited collection of my most memorable journeys. I hope my stories will inspire you to get off the couch and throw the clicker out the window. It opens with my whitewater rafting trip down the Tatshenshini River, a voyage that turned me into a raving environmentalist. "Not Enough Said for Solitude" and "Stepping Outside of the Big Box," set in the American Southwest, both encourage you to slow down and connect with nature. Eco-alerts were inserted where I saw something so detrimental to the environment taking place, I felt compelled to bring attention to it.

Covid-19 pulled the rug out from under travel, so I filled the year of the virus writing

Embrace of the Wild. Lady Isabella Lucy Bird has long been an inspirational character in my life. Her descriptions of riding with wild abandon in Hawai'i and in the Rocky Mountains made me want to fly with her. Writing her story allowed me to be in my two favorite places on my favorite mode of transport while being self-isolated. I pretended that I was enjoying a writer's residency in the Rocky Mountain National Forest outside of Estes Park.

If you enjoyed *Embrace of the Wild*, please take a moment to review it on Amazon or Goodreads. Reader feedback is the life blood of authors. Information about all my books is on my Amazon profile page or on my site www. LindaBallouAuthor.com.

www.LostAngelAdventures.com is dedicated to my travel books and articles.

Join me for my latest updates on Facebook.

Lightning Source UK Ltd.
Milton Keynes UK
UKHW022010041222
413380UK00009B/157